SIN'S DAUGHTER

A SINS SERIES NOVELLA

EVE SILVER

BOOK DESCRIPTION
SIN'S DAUGHTER

Sin's Daughter is a Sins Series novella that can be read at any point in the series.

For fans of Egyptian mythology, magic, a kick-butt heroine, a dark demigod hero, and enemies to lovers.

Library Journal raves the Sins Series is "...dark, seductive, and sexy as sin."

Cursed with immortality, driven into a nomadic life on the fringes of society to escape those who hunt her, Amber Hale has learned the bitter lesson that she can never grow close to anyone. Never love. Only once did she break her own rules. And her lover, Kai Warin, paid for her mistake with his life. For decades, she's been numb with grief.

Now, confronted by a soul reaper—an agent of one of the most powerful of the Underworld deities—with Kai's face, she must acknowledge the likelihood that he betrayed her... to the Lord of Evil himself.

Forced into an uneasy alliance and plagued by the unwanted yearning between them, Kai and Amber must work together to elude the dark forces hunting them both...

Join Eve's VIP Reader Group and get a FREE book!

Follow Eve on Bookbub!

ALSO BY EVE SILVER

Dark Gothic Series

(Books in this series can be read in any order)

Dark Desires

His Dark Kiss

Dark Prince

His Wicked Sins

Seduced by a Stranger

Dark Embrace

The Sins Series

Sins of the Heart (Book 1)

Sins of the Soul (Book 2)

Sins of the Flesh (Book 3)

Body of Sin (Book 4)

Sin's Daughter (Novella, can be read at any point in the series)

Northern Waste Series

(Eve Silver writing as Eve Kenin)

Driven (Book 1)

Frozen (Book 1.5)

Hidden (Book 2)

Compact of Sorcerers Series

Demon's Kiss (Book 1)

Demon's Hunger (Book 2)

Trinity Blue (short story)

The Game Series (Young Adult)

Rush (Book 1)

Push (Book 2)

Crash (Book 3)

Join Eve's VIP Reader Group for the latest info about contests, new releases and more! www.EveSilver.net

Follow Eve on Bookbub!

www.evesilver.net

SIN'S DAUGHTER

e-ISBN: 978-1-988674-07-0

print ISBN: 978-1-988674-11-7

NOTE TO READER

I am the master of my fate:
I am the captain of my soul.
—from *Invictus* by William Ernest Henley

PROLOGUE

The Underworld, the Territory of Sutekh

Fifty years ago

Kai Warin stood on a sandstone gallery shrouded in preternatural silence. He definitely wasn't on Pfeiffer Beach anymore. The lack of sand and waves and sky gave it away. He couldn't remember leaving the beach, couldn't remember how he got here.

And where was here?

A glance over the balustrade revealed an endless line of people snaking into the distance, all of them looking straight ahead. No one spoke. Not even a whisper. Nothing about this place was familiar. Everything about it was disturbing.

He had a feeling that clicking his heels together three times and wishing for home wouldn't take him back.

As he drew a deep breath, pain knifed through him,

making him gasp, stealing his thoughts. He slapped one hand against the wall, steadying himself, and pressed the other to his chest.

Warm. Sticky.

When he drew his hand away it was covered in blood.

Fear bit at him. Not for himself. For Amber. He pictured her, light brown hair tousled by the wind, eyes bright as she looked at him. And then she was gone. Fading like morning mist under the glare of the warming sun.

Was she safe? She had to be safe.

The thought brought anger shimmering over him in hot waves, and for a second, he just stood there, disoriented. He was angry at *her*, and that made no sense.

He closed his eyes.

Red lipstick on the bathroom mirror.

Amber liked to do little things like that, leave a lipstick note on the mirror, draw a heart in the dust on the window of his car, bake his favorite cookies in the wee hours of the night while he slept so he woke up to a plate of them waiting on the kitchen table. She liked to surprise him.

She'd written two words on the mirror: *Pfeiffer Beach.* Their private place. She called it the most beautiful beach in the world. He'd kissed her there for the first time. Weeks later, he'd brought blankets and made love to her there under the stars.

He'd grinned when he'd seen her note and then he'd made his way to the beach. But this time, it hadn't been Amber there waiting for him. It had been...

He stared at his bloody hand for a long moment.

He couldn't remember.

He closed his fist and felt the slippery warmth of his own blood. Except...he didn't. He shot a look at his hand.

There was no blood. He slapped his palm to his chest. Still no blood.

The gallery spun around him, or maybe he spun as the gallery stood still. Again, he reached for the wall to hold himself up, but there was no wall. Or maybe there was no hand.

He didn't know how long he stood there. He felt like he floated, like he was made of air.

Finally, he staggered forward and as he approached the tall wooden doors before him swung open. Pausing, he searched for any hint of movement, any threat.

"Come," a voice bid him, low, commanding.

He stayed where he was, framed in the doorway. The room was vast with pale stone walls and floor, an arched ceiling high above. Tall columns ran the length and at the far end was a man sitting on a raised dais. Beyond the dais were open doors, the light at the man's back, leaving him a dark silhouette.

A breeze stirred and Kai smelled flowers, the scent not unpleasant—

"Lotus blossoms," the voice clarified in a flat, bored tone.

"What do you want?" Kai asked, cutting to the chase.

Again, the pain in his chest came, twisting him in knots. He couldn't breathe. Couldn't think. Could barely stand. In his mind's eye, he saw muzzle flashes from at least three weapons.

He'd been shot.

The memory of lying in the sand with the sound of the waves and the wind flowed over him, then ebbed, slipping from his grasp. He stood, panting, sweating, trying to wrangle the memories into something that made sense.

"Do you understand?" the voice asked.

"No."

Again, the scene played out in his thoughts, as though he were standing on one side, watching. Sand. Wind. Waves. The star-dotted sky overhead. The sounds of gunshots. A body jerking, falling, lying still.

His body.

Pain blossomed in his chest, stronger this time. He cried out and fell to his knees.

"Do you understand now?" the voice asked.

"Yes." He did. He was dead, and this sure as fuck wasn't heaven. Emotions buffeted him: regret, sadness, anger, fear.

"Amber," he said, far more afraid for her than he was for himself.

"The woman remains Topworld," the voice said. Or did it? Kai had the impression he was hearing words that hadn't actually been spoken, words that were only in his mind.

Topworld. He took a second to figure that out. "You mean, she's still alive."

"Yes."

"And this is...the Underworld?"

"Yes."

"Hell?" He wouldn't be surprised. He wasn't evil—at least, he didn't think he was. But there were things he'd done in his life, things he'd done in the name of his country in a place far from home that definitely couldn't be called good.

"The Underworld has many names, many parts, many rulers," the voice replied. "This is my territory."

Kai pressed the sides of his balled fists to his forehead. He'd died. He was here and Amber was there, back in the real world. And she was alone. He hated that, hated that he'd broken his promise to her.

"Tell me about your family. Brothers? Sisters?" he'd asked one night as they lay naked and sated.

Shadows had clouded her eyes.

"No one," she'd replied. "My mother and I..." She'd looked away, but not before he'd seen the sheen of moisture on her lashes.

"Not a good relationship?"

She'd shaken her head. "It was a wonderful relationship. She was a wonderful mother," she'd whispered. "She died."

"I'm sorry. Your dad?"

"I never knew him." She'd swiped the back of her hand across her eyes, wiping away the tears, and then she'd looked at him, her expression calm. "I have no one. It's better that way."

Better? "You have me," he'd said, and offered a cocky smile. "Forever. I promise."

But that had only made the shadows in her eyes grow darker. "Forever is such a long time," she'd whispered and laid her fingers across his lips. "Don't make promises of forever."

And now he was dead. He'd left her. They hadn't had forever.

"You waste your concern, Kai Warin," the man's voice came again.

Kai dropped his hands and lifted his head. "What does that mean?"

"You waste thoughts on the woman you left behind. Think. *Remember.*"

A surge of rage swelled. So much anger, all of it aimed at Amber.

He saw a slash of red lipstick on the mirror, *Pfeiffer Beach* written in Amber's distinctive hand. He'd always teased her about it, her perfect penmanship, like she'd learned how to form letters in a time when penmanship was an art.

He pushed to his feet, shaking, wary, and stood swaying a moment before the voice came to him again.

"You understand that she sent you there? You understand what she did?"

Rage. Pain. Disbelief.

"No."

"She sent you to die."

"No."

Lipstick on the mirror. Pfeiffer Beach. But she hadn't been waiting for him there.

"You don't know what you're talking about," he said.

"Do I not?" The man made a languid shrug.

Kai took two steps forward, hands balled into fists at his sides. Only then did he realize they weren't alone. There was someone else there, sitting in a dim corner. A man, young, blond, handsome. He rose and stepped forward. The man on the dais glanced at him and said, "No need, Lokan," then he looked back at Kai.

"Come, Kai Warin. Come to me. Hear what I offer." The words were spoken in a soft tone, cajoling, kind, but Kai heard them for what they were: not a request but an order.

"Do I have a choice?" he asked.

"There is always a choice. Yours is between eternal life and annihilation." A pause, then, "Choose wisely."

1

___

SAN FRANCISCO, CALIFORNIA

PRESENT DAY

THEY WERE HUNTING HER. AMBER HALE forced herself to stay perfectly still, to think, to plan. There were at least three of them out there. Maybe more. They had her cornered. She needed to get out, get away. But not yet, not until she made certain they couldn't follow.

She rolled across the bed and came down on the opposite side, pushed up on all fours and lifting her gaze to the open bedroom door.

No one there. Yet.

But they would come. Any moment now, they would come.

The thump of the bass and the drums carried up through the floor, through her knees, and up her thighs, pounding in time with her runaway pulse. The music was a benefit—and curse—of living above a bar. Free concerts. The good, and the bad. Some nights, she was grateful for the invention of silicone earplugs.

Tonight, she was grateful that the noise meant no one was likely to hear the shots.

Her heart slammed against her ribs. She dragged the mattress down, tipping it onto its side to form a wall between her and the door. Then she shoved her hand into the hole in the box spring and grabbed the gun. A Taurus Millennium Pro with a suppressor. Light and small, it nestled neatly in her palm.

Guns weren't her thing, but she'd long ago learned that needs must when the devil drives. So, she'd bought a gun and practiced regularly. She could hit what she aimed at, and in the event her target was human, she'd be aiming for head or heart.

She shivered. She wasn't certain that what was about to come through that door was human. And she wasn't certain if she could really pull the trigger.

Shoot only if you mean it, and if there is no other choice. The memory hurtled at her, stinging like a stone churned up against a windshield. It had been decades, but she could almost hear Kai's voice as he'd said that, see the look in his eyes. All business. He was the one who'd first put a gun in her hand. It was one of the things that had convinced her that he meant it when he said he loved her, the fact that he'd insisted she learn how to defend herself.

But he hadn't loved her. He'd betrayed her—

No. She would not think about him.

Ever since she'd come back to San Francisco, thoughts of Kai had surfaced too often for comfort. She'd loved him with all her heart and soul.

She'd been a fool.

Those memories had no place in this moment. Not if she hoped to escape.

Scuttling back along the hardwood floor, she jammed herself into the corner. The mattress offered a whisper of protection, but it also blocked her sight line. She'd known that, of course, because she'd run this drill dozens of times, just in case. The first time around, she'd realized her view of any approaching threat sucked. So, she'd angled the full-length mirror to give her a clear perspective of half the living room and the front door of the apartment.

She stared at the mirror now, both hands circling the butt of the gun as she thumbed off the safety and held her place.

Silver linings, my little love. Look hard enough and you'll always find one. The words reached across the barrier of time. There had been no silver lining the night Kai died. Only heartbreak and horror and despair. And layered on that, the awareness that he'd sold her out, and she would never know why.

She knew why she was thinking about him now though, thinking about that night. That was the last time she'd been cornered like this, the closest she'd ever come to being caught. It had been decades ago, but it felt like yesterday.

Seconds scraped past, too slow for comfort. Her skin prickled. Her mouth felt like she'd been drinking sand. A part of her just wanted to bolt, but that would only make things worse. She'd already let them get too close. If she ran, they'd follow. If she ran, she might not be fast enough. If she ran, they might catch her. She needed to wait right here, wait until they came. And then she needed to kill them.

Hunters, her mother had called them. They'd found her many times over the years and she'd escaped every time. But they'd only ever come this close the night Kai had sent her to Coit Tower.

Tonight, the ones that had come for her were playing cat and mouse.

She felt like one hell of a clueless mouse.

She'd run right into their trap. She'd ignored her sixth sense. On her way home, there had been that split second when she'd paused on Market, the streetlights casting the Flat Iron Building bright and almost white against the black of the night sky, the moon full and round. A breathtaking scene.

But that wasn't the reason she'd stopped. She'd been wary of the three guys across the street. They had passed her, heading off along Sutter. She'd watched them and, once they were a block away, dismissed them. Until she'd seen them again in the line to get into the bar below her apartment.

In her dictionary, there was no such thing as happenstance.

They were hunters, and she'd let them get too close. Running would only make them hungry to follow. Getting upstairs and getting her gun gave her a better chance. If she ran and they followed, they might catch her. If she hunkered down and waited for them, killed them before she ran, they wouldn't be able to follow.

She kept her breathing even as she stared at the reflection of the door in the mirror. They were taking too long. They might not realize she'd spotted them. She doubted they'd expect her to be armed.

They hadn't been looking her way as she'd unlocked her door and headed upstairs, but in her gut, she'd known. They were aware of her every movement. They would come, and she'd made herself an easy mark.

It wasn't the first time she'd slipped up, just the first time in recent memory. After Kai, she'd been so damned careful.

Keeping the gun level now, she eased one hand under the bed and closed her fingers around the straps of the small black knapsack she always kept packed and ready. Change of clothes. Cash. Fake ID. First-aid kit.

There was nothing else in the small apartment that couldn't be left behind. Time to move forward, move on. She'd stayed too long already.

In fact, she should never have returned to San Francisco. She'd left her heart here once before, and she'd been a sentimental moron to return. There were plenty of cities in this world. From here on out she'd stick to the ones she'd never been to before.

She slid the straps of the backpack over her shoulders, one then the other, keeping a close watch on the front door. The window to her left was an alternate exit. But they could have left a guard down there.

She wasn't of a mind to shoot someone while the line of bar patrons milling on the sidewalk watched. Witnesses were never a good thing.

So, she waited, gun in hand, pulse racing, and she hoped to hell she was making the right call.

They took so long that she almost allowed herself to hope that they weren't coming. Then, in the mirror, she saw the apartment door vibrate and bulge inward. Her stomach turned a sickening roll. The door flew open, the old wood around the lock splintering under repeated impact, the screws of the double chains she'd installed pulling free. The accompanying crash was all but obliterated by the truly lousy rendition of "Devil Inside" carrying up from below.

She could barely breathe. Her chest felt like it had a

metal band around it, being drawn ever tighter. But the gun in her hand was steady.

Up on its side, the mattress formed a protective wall of springs and foam. She didn't dare lean to see past it because then they might catch sight of her. Instead, pulse racing, she watched in the mirror as the first guy came through the door. He was layered in muscle, and he had the cold, flat look of someone who hunted often and well. His long hair was greased back from his face and he wore a bunch of heavy gold chains around his neck.

She didn't move. She just watched him and waited. He took his time, pausing just inside the door to look around. He was followed by two others. Taller. Leaner. Younger. One of them hadn't been there earlier when she'd seen them downstairs. Which meant there were more than three.

Were they human? Or were they...like her?

She'd only ever been this close to those who hunted her that night when Kai had lured her to Coit Tower with roses and a note. Her mother's warnings had sufficed to keep her on her toes and always ready to bolt.

Her earliest memories were of her mother holding her close and telling her terrible stories of the men who chased them.

"How will I recognize the bad men, Mama?"

"You will feel it here, in your heart, in your soul. When you see them, run. Think of nothing and no one else. Just run. Hide. Be safe."

If she had run when she first spotted them on Market, she'd be far away by now. But the contents of her backpack would have been forfeit, and replacing ID was never easy. Too, the hunters would be alive to follow. So maybe it had been a mistake not to run, and maybe it hadn't. But she needed to stop beating herself up about that.

Everyone made mistakes. She could only hope this one didn't prove disastrous for her.

The music from downstairs amped up another notch. She felt the beat clear through to her bones.

The guy with the slicked-back hair shot a quick look at each of the other two, then he gestured toward the kitchen, and one of them headed in that direction. That meant he was out of her sight line. She didn't like that.

She eased forward, risking discovery, but widening the mirror's reflected view.

Extending two fingers toward the open bedroom door, the leader sent the third guy heading in her direction and she saw the glint of a knife in his hand. She didn't know why it surprised her. They were monsters, hunters who would do whatever it took to catch her. But while she could remember nets and batons and lariats from every previous near miss, she couldn't recall ever having seen them with knives or guns. Not even that night at Coit Tower.

The leader turned. His gaze met Amber's in the mirror, then flicked to her gun. For a millisecond, everything froze. Then he opened his mouth, and she knew he called out though the pounding music made his words indecipherable.

Fear writhed and twisted inside her, a beast on a short chain.

Do anything to escape them. Anything. Her mother's warnings uttered thousands of times over the years coalesced into an icy ball in her gut.

Lunging for the door to the bedroom, the leader pulled a gun from the holster beneath his arm as he moved. The guy with the knife was a step ahead of him.

The weapons were a clear statement that they were willing to kill her. Which either meant that they could take what they wanted from her corpse, or they knew that, for her, *dead* had an unusual meaning.

Either way, she had no intention of offering an easy mark.

Amber surged to her feet and fired halfway through the exhale. A shot to the head. The first bullet went in just above the bridge of the younger guy's nose. The second took him high on the right cheek.

Time froze. Bile crawled up the back of her throat. She'd trained for years, but she'd never actually fired at a person before.

The hunter just stood there, staring at her. Then he dropped to the floor as though his bones had liquefied all at once.

Panting, she realized he had been the only thing standing between her and the leader's gun. Now there was nothing.

Not that she feared death. Having been through it three times already, she was a fair hand at it now. The first time she died she was five, run down by a wagon. She woke to find herself lying on a wooden table in a pool of blood. She'd opened her eyes and sat up and the women standing around her had screamed and crossed themselves. Her mother had burst through the caterwauling circle and bundled her up and they had run, leaving everything behind except the clothes on their backs. The women and men of her village, those who had known her since birth, who had dried her tears and fed her sweets and laughed at her antics, now wanted to tie her to a stake and burn her alive.

That was the first time that Amber had understood that she was different and that the hunters her mother spoke of wanted her because of those differences. Her mother had sworn that if the hunters got her, what would follow would be more terrible than she could ever imagine. To this day, Amber had never doubted her, and it was the knowledge that they wanted something from her—some intangible, unnamed thing—that made panic curdle in her gut.

Her mother had refused to tell her what that thing was, no matter how many years passed and how many times they had to run. Her mother was dead now. Buried. So, it was too late for answers.

And Amber was alone, a freak who couldn't age or die, whose every injury healed within hours.

She dropped to her knees as a bullet grazed the edge of the mattress, sending bits of foam and cloth in all directions.

Going down flat on her belly, she fired straight ahead under the bed, a clean shot through the leader's ankle.

But he didn't fall.

His feet left the floor as he dived overtop the box spring, leaving spots of blood dotted with shiny white chips of bone behind on the pale wood floor. His momentum sent the mattress toppling against the wall.

Amber rolled out of the way and surged to her feet to dart around the foot of the bed. From the corner of her eye, she caught movement in the mirror. A fourth guy coming through the apartment door? Or was it just the third one moving around?

No time to find out.

She spun to face slicked-back hair and gold chains and a gun.

Their eyes met.

Something hit her left shoulder, a dull thud. But she held her place.

Aim. Exhale. Squeeze.

Her bullet went in just above his left eye.

Blood and tissue splattered her beige wall.

She fired again. The insurance shot. More blood. More splatter.

Don't look. Don't think about it.

She felt dizzy. Sick. She'd never been this close. Never had to kill anyone. Never had to actually fire her gun at anything that lived and breathed.

Now, she'd killed two men.

She turned and looked to the open bedroom door, expecting to see the last guy framed in the entry.

No one there.

She had the horrible feeling that it was only the element of surprise that had saved her so far. She doubted they'd expected her to fight back. Or to have a gun.

The element of surprise had been expended.

She shook her head to clear the buzzing, then pressed her hand to her shoulder. It came away streaked with blood.

Not good. Just because she would heal, that didn't mean that blood loss didn't affect her or that pain didn't make her want to howl.

Glancing around, she saw the purple silk scarf she'd bought months ago because she'd liked the color. It was draped where she'd left it, over the bedside lampshade. She grabbed it and wrapped her shoulder as tight as she could manage, tying off the ends using one hand and her teeth, her gaze locked on the bedroom door.

There was no outcry from the bar below, which meant that either no one had heard the shots, or they'd decided it was all part of the show.

But the guy in the other room had to have heard them.

Which meant he was forewarned. He knew she had a weapon. And he knew she would use it.

Maybe that was why he hadn't come tearing in here. He was waiting out there. Waiting for her to make a mistake.

She glanced at the mirror. The angle was wrong. She couldn't see the living room, just the splintered front door and the entryway. She couldn't see the third hunter, and she didn't know if there was a fourth.

Pressing tight to the wall, she peered around the bedroom door, her palms slick, a trickle of cold sweat snaking between her breasts.

There *was* a fourth. She caught a glimpse of his back, his raised arm and his fingers curled around the third hunter's throat. She had a fleeting impression of a dark jacket and dark hair and not much else before she jerked back and stood with one palm flat against the wall and her chest heaving.

Were they fighting among themselves? She couldn't credit that. More likely, the late arrival was a new player entirely. The rules of the game had just shifted and she was left reeling.

She needed to get out of here. And if she were smart, she'd kill both those men out there to make certain they didn't follow. The thought almost made her dry heave. It was one thing to kill in self-defense, quite another to shoot a man in the back.

Carefully, she twisted and leaned to look out once more.

The band downstairs ended the set, leaving an instant of comparative quiet.

The man in the black jacket tightened his hold on the hunter's throat. Then he formed a claw with the fingers of his left hand and rammed them through the hunter's chest.

Amber pressed the back of her fist against her mouth as the sound of ribs snapping filled the silence.

The hunter's mouth opened in a soundless scream, as

though the breath had been stolen from his lungs. The fist-sized hole in his chest might explain that.

She couldn't move. Couldn't look away. Could only watch in horror as the guy with his back to her rooted around in the hunter's chest and tore out his heart with a vicious yank.

A crimson arc sprayed the wall.

He held the still-pulsing heart in his fist, blood dripping to the floor, then he shoved it into...something...a pocket? A pouch? She couldn't see from this angle.

Move. She needed to move. But her feet wouldn't obey her silent command. Terror held her rooted.

There was blood everywhere. The floor. The wall. The hunter's clothing.

Maybe she made a sound. Or maybe he just sensed her. But he lowered his chin and turned his head, not enough so she could see his face, but enough that she could hear him in the relative quiet as the band geared up for their next set.

"I'm not here for you," he said, his voice a low rasp that scraped her nerve endings raw.

She took a step to the side, then froze as a greasy black *thing* oozed from the gaping hole in the hunter's chest and curled around his killer's wrist, then inched up his arm like a slug made of thick, oily smoke.

"Go," he ordered and turned his face back toward his prey.

He released his hold on the hunter's throat. The body collapsed to the ground, the black slug rising like a cloud of putrid smoke to hover above the killer's shoulder, held there by a bright thread of light.

Amber willed her feet to move. But she managed only a shuffling slide, her legs shaking so hard she could barely stay on her feet.

Then it was too late.

She heard him inhale sharply.

He turned, his movements slow, and Amber's world ground to an abrupt, stomach-churning halt. Close-cropped dark hair. High cheekbones. Eyes dark and framed by thick, curling lashes. Dark stubble shading his jaw.

His expression was flat and cold, mirroring none of the incredulity that cascaded through her.

Kai.

It couldn't be.

He was dead.

That thought forced a bubble of hysterical laughter up her throat, and she choked it back. She knew better than anyone that dying was relative.

But...Kai? She'd visited his grave. Only once, right after he'd died. That was all she'd dared because that grave would have been the first place the hunters looked.

No...twice. She'd been an idiot. She'd taken flowers last week. On his birthday. Gerbera daisies. Because he'd always given her Gerberas; she loved the bright colors. God, how could she have been so stupid? He'd sold her out to the hunters and she'd come back fifty years later to visit his grave in a moment of melancholy loneliness.

That was what had started this. She'd gone to Kai's grave and even all these years later, they must have been watching.

She stared at him now. The hard planes and angles of his face caught the light filtering through the window that overlooked the street.

His eyes held hers, and she saw nothing there. Not love. Not hate. Perhaps not even recognition.

With a gasp, she fell back. This was Kai, but not Kai. Not the man she'd known.

Her gaze dipped to his blood-drenched hand. Clearly not the man she'd known.

The band started up again, the bass pounding through her, or maybe that was only the rushing of her pulse.

"Amber." His lips shaped her name, but she didn't hear the word.

Her throat constricted and her heart gave a painful jerk.

She backed up, turned, and saw only a blur as he moved to block her route to the door. He'd moved so damn fast.

"Let me pass," she said, uncertain if he could even hear her above the music.

He only stared at her, saying nothing. Her gaze flicked to the dead hunter who lay in a pool of blood, his chest ripped open, then to the dark, amorphous mass floating above Kai's shoulder.

"Are you one of them?" she asked.

He flicked a glance at the dead man. "No."

"Let me go," she said. "Before more come."

"No."

What if he was lying? What if he *was* one of them? Fear congealed in her gut. She shifted to one side. He mirrored her movement. She shifted to the opposite side. He did the same, blocking her way.

"Kai, let me go. I need to go. You don't understand. I can't let you take me—" Panic swallowed her words. He was one of them, a hunter, and he wasn't letting her go.

She would be taken. Captured. What terrible things would they do to her? Her mother's warnings rang in her ears. The terror in her mother's eyes was a memory she could never evade.

She swallowed against the knot that clogged her throat.

Kai was alive. He was here.

He'd killed a hunter.

But that didn't mean he wasn't one of them. He could simply be working for a different team.

She felt like she was choking, dying, the world spinning. She'd never before considered the possibility that there was more than one group hunting her.

"Let me go," she said again.

He reached for her.

"I'm sorry," she whispered. Then she raised her hand, pulled the trigger and shot him through the heart.

2

KAI CAUGHT HER ON THE STAIRS. HE GOT ONE ARM AROUND Amber's waist, lifted her clear off her feet and slapped his other palm over her mouth. She struggled and kicked and clawed at his skin, tearing bloody runnels.

His chest felt like it was on fire. Christ. She'd shot him. In the heart.

It was kind of fitting if he thought about it. The only thing more apt would have been if she reached inside him and ripped the damned thing clean out.

Amber.

She was alive. She was here. She was in his arms. Struggling, kicking, ready to try to kill him if he gave her the chance.

She hadn't aged a day.

What the fuck?

He'd lost count of the number of nights he'd dreamed of her, ached for her. Fantasized about tearing her lying, deceitful heart from her breast. And he'd lost count of the number of days he'd forced himself not to go looking for her.

"Fifty years," he snarled. "Fifty fucking years and the first thing you do is shoot me?" Of all the things to say, all the things to ask, that was the best he could come up with? But with the band in the bar below playing loud enough to shake the walls, she probably hadn't heard him anyway.

As she struggled in his arms, the scent of her hair drifted to him. She wore it exactly the same, loose to her shoulders, light brown, tipped in gold. He gave in to temptation and lowered his face. She smelled the same and he wanted to bury his face in her neck, breathe deep, and lose himself in the memories of everything they'd once had.

Had. Past tense. Key concept here.

Glancing at the door at the base of the stairs, he tightened his grip as she elbowed him in the side. He shifted his weight, trapping her between his chest and the wall of the stairway, preventing her from moving the hand that held the gun. Not that she could kill him. But he felt pain and, having one bullet in him already, he wasn't anxious for more.

He wrenched the gun from her grasp, checked the safety and shoved the barrel into his waistband so it lay against his spine. Not ideal, but it would do for the moment.

She struggled and writhed as he half dragged, half carried her back up the stairs, not stopping at her door, but heading higher, toward the roof. It would be quieter up there and, for the moment, safe enough.

Pain exploded, bright and hot, as she gave a particularly violent wrench that rammed her elbow into the hole in his chest. He was tempted to return the favor, to dig his fingers into the wound in her shoulder.

In the end, he didn't. Couldn't.

Wouldn't.

Whatever he'd become, he couldn't hurt her. Not on purpose and not like that.

But he kept a tight grip on her as he climbed the steps, refusing to give an inch. He hadn't come here for her, but now that he had her, he wasn't about to let her go until he got some answers.

He'd come to San Francisco on Sutekh's orders. Lokan, Sutekh's youngest son, had been murdered. Sutekh wanted the killer, and everyone in his ranks was on high alert. Anything out of the ordinary was suspect, and a slew of Asmodeus's grunts heading en masse from their home turf in Toronto to San Francisco was definitely out of the ordinary. Whatever the job was that needed to get done, why not just use a local crew?

Sutekh had sent Kai to find out, and to harvest the dark-soul of one man in particular, one who owed Sutekh a debt. Kai glanced at the dark mass hovering above his shoulder. One task down.

Now if he could get some information out of Amber, maybe he could complete the second task and get answers about Asmodeus because it was her apartment Asmodeus's men had headed for, and from all appearances, she'd been their target.

Whether that had anything to do with Lokan's murder, he couldn't say. Not yet.

He hauled Amber onto the roof and kicked the door shut behind him. The sounds of the bar and the street and the traffic carried to them, but it was far quieter up here than it had been below. And they were alone.

Amber jerked in his grasp, and he drew her tighter against him, resting his lips against her ear.

"What's the deal, Amber?" he asked, her name melting on his tongue. He felt her shiver. "You're here. You're alive. And you don't look a minute older than the last time I saw you...which was what? Fifty years ago?" He paused. "I'm going to take my hand away from your mouth. Don't scream. You never know what kind of vermin might come running."

She gave a spare nod and he let his hand drop but still held her trapped against him.

"I could ask you the same thing," she said, struggling against him. "You died fifty years ago."

She'd sent him to die. Lucky for him, things had worked out different than she'd planned.

"I did die. I just didn't stay that way."

"I just shot you through the heart. Why aren't you dead now?"

"Disappointed?" Circling both her wrists with one hand, he turned her to face him. Her hair tumbled forward in tousled, loose curls. There was a purple scarf tied around her shoulder and he could smell her blood. He wondered how badly she was hurt. Then he wondered why he cared. "Why did you shoot me?"

"I won't be taken." She glared at him, defiant.

"Taken? I told you I wasn't here for you. I told you to go."

"That was before you turned around and saw me."

True. Once he'd seen her, there'd been no way he'd let her go. "I don't *take* people, Amber. I kill them."

She stared up at him, holding his gaze. Her defiance melted away, replaced by a calm mask that hid her thoughts and emotions. He couldn't read her expression, couldn't tell what she was thinking.

Finally, she said, "You're not him."

"Who?"

"My Kai."

Her words turned him inside out. "Your Kai died." He kept his tone cold and flat. "And I think the woman he knew as Amber never existed. Not the way he thought she did."

She frowned. "You know you're referring to yourself in the third person. That can't be a good sign."

He huffed a laugh. He couldn't help it.

She swayed and closed her eyes for a second. The scarf she'd tied around her shoulder was drenched with her blood. He needed to see how badly she was hurt. He told himself it was because he wouldn't get answers if she was dead.

But first, he needed to make a point.

"Open your eyes, Amber."

She obeyed.

He pulled her gun from his waist, lifted it so she had a clear view, closed his hand on the barrel, and crushed it. Her eyes widened. Point made.

"Now stay still and let me check this." He let go of her wrists, took the silk scarf between his hands and tore it in two.

He hadn't been gentle. He suspected he'd hurt her. But she only watched him, wary.

Then she swayed again, as though overwhelmed by the events of the night or her wound or the fact that he'd risen from the dead. Maybe she was. But he didn't trust anything about her. Maybe she was just planning to throw him off guard.

"Don't faint," he ordered. *Don't die,* he thought.

"I won't."

She reached toward the hole she'd put in his chest, stopping just short of touching him, then dropped her hand to her side. "What are you?" she asked, and her gaze flicked to the darksoul bobbing at his shoulder. So, she could see that. Interesting.

"What am I?" No reason to lie when the truth would do. "I'm a reaper." He cocked a brow and looked at the skin showing through the blood-crusted hole in her shirt. It was healing already, pink puckered flesh that looked like a month-old scar rather than a fresh wound. "I share, you share. What are you?"

Two parallel lines appeared between her brows. He remembered that frown. How many times had he reached out and smoothed it away?

"You're a grim reaper?" she asked, sidling away from him. One step. Two. He let her go because there really was nowhere for her *to* go. He stood between her and the stairs. "Like an angel of death?"

He blinked. He'd thought she'd know what he was talking about. After all, she'd been the one to set in motion the events that landed him in Sutekh's greeting chamber.

"A *soul* reaper," he said, watching her carefully.

The words didn't appear to mean a damned thing to her.

"You're not a hunter?" She paused. "Like them?" She made a gesture down toward her apartment, which reminded him... He pulled out his phone and hesitated for a second, trying to decide who to call for a clean-up. Too many bodies. Likely to raise too many questions if he left them to be found by mortals.

He chose a number. Malthus Krayl answered. Kai figured that if he needed a favor, Mal was his best choice. He was high up in the ranks, one of Sutekh's sons. He was easy-going and always ready for anything. But he wouldn't ask the questions that Sutekh's second-in-command, Gahiji, would ask if Kai called him instead. Besides, cellular reach didn't extend to the Underworld and that was where Gahiji preferred to lurk while Mal spent his off time in Topworld.

Amber waited until he finished the call, then asked, "Are you a hunter?"

"I work for Sutekh," he said, and when she didn't react,

he continued. "Set. Seteh. Lord of the desert. Lord of chaos. God of storms. God of darkness. The Underworld überlord of chaos and evil."

"Underworld," she said, latching on to that one point. She looked up at the darksoul he'd harvested, bobbing somewhere to the left of his head. She took another couple of steps away from him. "You're a soul reaper, so...is that a soul?"

"A darksoul. It's a meal for Sutekh. He has an army of us harvesting for him."

"A meal?"

Kai offered a close-lipped smile. "He ingests darksouls. He feeds off evil."

She shivered, though the night was warm.

"What about—" she pointed at the pouch he'd thrust the heart into "—that?"

"The heart? It's an offering for Osiris. Helps keep Osiris and Sutekh from each other's throats." That was the simplest explanation. He wasn't about to try and explain the intricacies of a six-thousand-year-old cease-fire or the fact that Sutekh had once murdered Osiris and hacked his body to bits.

"How—"

"No," he cut her off. "We're trading answers. I showed you mine. Time to show me yours. You can see the darksoul. That's proof positive that you aren't human." Maybe she never had been. He supposed that of all the things he could hold against her, that really wasn't one of them, since he wasn't human anymore himself.

"I'm human," she whispered, crossing her arms across her middle like she was holding herself together by a thread.

He closed the distance between them and yanked aside

the neckline of her shirt, baring the healing wound in her shoulder. "Right."

With a glare, she jerked away and retreated.

"You heal mighty fast. You haven't aged a day in fifty years." He matched her stride for stride, one forward for each step she took backward until she was at the edge of the roof, her legs and ass pressed against the low wall. In the distance, a siren wailed. Sounds from the street below wafted up: a woman's laughter, a man's voice, the sound of the music, louder when someone opened the door to enter the bar, softer when it swung shut.

"What do you owe Asmodeus?" he asked, not that he really needed that information. She wasn't his concern. He should just take his harvest, open a portal, and leave. So why did he take yet another step forward leaving only inches between them?

Because he wanted answers. That was the only reason.

He could tell himself that a thousand times and he still wouldn't believe it.

"Asmodeus," she repeated, as though the name were a foreign flavor touching her tongue for the first time.

"Underworld deity," he clarified. "Demon of lust. He runs Topworld rackets. Drugs. Prostitutes. Given that those were his grunts we just terminated, I'm guessing you sold him something in exchange for eternal youth and life and then reneged on your deal. And now he's after you."

She shook her head. "Hunters are after me. Those were hunters."

"Hunters. Grunts. Call them whatever the hell you want. What do they want with you?"

"I don't know."

"You don't know what they want, but you know they're hunters? That they're hunting you?"

"Yes." Her answer was barely a whisper.

"Those grunts belong to Asmodeus. If they want you, then it's likely because *he* wants you. What did you promise him?"

"Nothing." She shook her head. "I never heard his name until you said it."

"Lie."

Her chin jutted forward. "Truth."

Kai didn't think she'd know what truth was even if it shot her through the heart.

Had Asmodeus been after her for all these years? That night on Pfeiffer Beach, had she seen Kai as her way out? Had she meant to trade a life for a life? His for hers? Thinking back on it, the men who'd killed him could well have belonged to Asmodeus.

For fifty years, he'd agonized over the answers, wanting to know *why.* He'd loved her. If she'd asked him, he would have died for her. But she hadn't asked. She'd just sent him to his death.

She looked at him, then looked away as she tucked her hair behind her ear. It didn't stay put. It fell forward again across her cheek. He was blindsided by a rush of memories. She was beautiful. Her brows were finely arched and winged up at the sides, her eyes light brown, flecked with gold. Unable to resist, he reached out and stroked the tumbled curl back from her cheek. He'd dreamed of her hair, her skin. The feel. The smell.

He leaned a little closer. Her lips parted. He knew the shape of them—the lower slightly fuller than the upper. Knew the feel of them. The taste.

"I saved your life in there," he said softly. "The least you can do is give me an honest answer. What do you owe

Asmodeus? And don't pretend you don't know what I'm talking about."

For an endless second, they just stood there, connected by the tips of his fingers where they rested on the arc of her cheek and by memories and history and a fine humming tension that sparked the night air.

"I saved my own life," she said, flinching away from his touch. He dropped his hand and followed her gaze to his fingers. They were smeared with blood—maybe his, maybe hers, maybe the blood of the grunt he'd ripped open—and he'd transferred some to her skin. Probably best not to tell her that.

With a shudder, she scrubbed the heel of her palm against her cheek, then stared at the blood that was now on her hand. Her gaze slowly returned to his.

"And I don't know what you're talking about." The words were low and emphatic like she was pouring her will into them. "I've never met Asmodeus. I made no deal with him. I owe him nothing."

"Do you think I believe you? I trusted you once." He huffed a short laugh. "You were always secretive, and I made excuses for that. Convinced myself you'd open up in time. Was there ever a word of truth in anything you told me?"

She didn't answer, but something flickered in her eyes. Guilt? Regret?

"I died on that beach," he said. "You got me killed."

"I got you—" She pressed her lips together and exhaled sharply through her nose, a sound of contempt. "You're not dead now."

"And neither are you. Explain that."

Indecision skittered across her features. And then she locked down, her expression closing. "You first."

She said it like she expected him to decline. But if tit for tat was what it took to get some answers out of her, he was fine with that.

"No problem. But not here." He tightened his grip on her wrist as he felt her muscles twitch. She meant to escape him. Good luck with that.

She cut him a glance through her lashes, her lips drawn taut and turned down at the corners, and he didn't like the way it made him feel. Like he was the bad guy. Which, actually, he was, thanks to her. Before she'd sent him out to die, he'd been a good guy. The help-an-old-lady-across-the-street, get-a-cat-out-of-a-tree, donate-blood kind of guy. Sort of.

Now, he was a rip-chests-open, harvest-darksouls, survival-of-the-fittest kind of guy. Sort of.

The thing about black or white was that there were a million shades of gray in between.

"Do you think there were only the three of those… grunts? Or are there more of them out there?" Amber asked, dipping her chin toward the edge of the roof.

He wasn't surprised. She'd always been practical. "You'll save your meltdown for later?"

"Not now. And not later," she said, and he knew it was true. Just one more thing that had made him fall in love with her all those years ago. She'd never been the type to pitch a fit. She'd been level-headed and practical and that had just made her quirky bits all the more endearing.

She pushed another errant wave back over her shoulder and he couldn't help but stare.

Love. Hate. Fine line in between. Whatever he felt for her now, it was colored by a heavy dose of lust.

The past slammed head-on into the present. He'd always been gentle back then. Careful. As if she were made of spun glass. He didn't want to be gentle now. He wanted to drag her against him and open his mouth on hers, taste her lips, her skin. He wanted to gather her hair and hold it in his fist while he pressed her down right here, on the roof, under the stars. He wanted to cover her, dominate her. Take her. Plunge into the heat of her. Make up for all the years of pain and loss.

Make her scream his name.

He wanted that with a fierceness that shocked him. Just from standing near her. It was all he could do not to give in and act on the need.

At the same time, he was acutely aware of the fact that whatever vengeance he'd dreamed about, he didn't want to hurt her. He just wanted to feel himself deep inside of her.

But only if she wanted him there.

Guess there was still a bit of the boy-scout in him buried somewhere under the layers of cold-blooded killer.

Amber froze, her eyes going wide, her pupils dilating. She sensed it, the thing inside him that pulsed and ached.

Scrubbing his palm along his jaw, he exhaled on a dark laugh.

"There are at least four more," he said, answering her earlier question, pretending that the beast lurking inside him wasn't a hair away from getting out. "Topworld grunts who work for Asmodeus, and they're a long way from home. The ones I recognize are all from his Toronto crew. Big Ralph's boys."

"You sound like a bad gangster movie." She lifted one hand in a gesture of futility. "I've never been to Toronto. I don't know anyone by the name of Big Ralph. Or Asmodeus."

She wanted to ask him about a million questions. He could see it in her expression. Instead, she just shook her head and said, "Let's go."

Decisive. Make her choice, follow through. He'd always liked that about her. It bothered him to realize he still did. What the hell was wrong with him? He'd played with this particular pack of matches before, and he'd been damned near incinerated. He ought to know better than to like anything about her.

"You're agreeable," he said. "Is it because you think I'm the lesser of evils?"

"Something like that. For now." She turned toward the stairs they'd taken to get up here.

He caught her wrist. "Wrong way. Go down those stairs and you walk right into their waiting arms," he said and dragged her back to the edge of the roof.

"I don't think—"

"Good," he cut her off. "Don't think. Just follow my lead." He let a mocking edge creep into his voice. "Unless you'd prefer to run into company." He dipped his chin toward the end of the street where two of Asmodeus's grunts lounged against a wall, the glow of their cigarettes surging each time they took a drag.

"How do you know they aren't just two guys out for a smoke?"

"I can see their faces."

She was silent for a second, digesting that. They were almost a block away.

"You're different now," she said. He thought she sounded wistful.

"Yeah." She had no idea.

The roof overlooked the back of the club. No one was down there.

She tugged at her trapped wrist but he didn't let her go.

Turning her to face him, he looped one arm tight around her waist and the other up along her spine.

"On three. One. Two—" And that was all the warning he gave her. With his fingers splayed across the base of her skull, he lifted her off her feet and jumped.

Her yelp was muffled in his shoulder. He had to give her credit; she didn't scream.

"Two stories," he said when they landed. "For me, that's like a hop." He kept his grip on her long enough for her to find her feet, and couldn't help but admire the fact that apart from a look that was vicious enough to gouge out eyes, she just nodded when he said, "This way."

They both knew that any more questions would have to wait until Asmodeus's grunts were left behind.

He stalked along the street, and when she wasn't fast enough, he grabbed hold of her wrist and pulled her along. He didn't need to look over his shoulder to know they were being followed. He felt it. And from the way she glanced back over her shoulder, he thought that maybe she did, too.

Yanking open the door to the public parking lot at the corner, he shoved her through ahead of him and barked, "Up."

She took the stairs two at a time, and he was close on her heels. Then he caught her wrist again, surged ahead, and dragged her through the door to P3. The band of pure energy that he'd used to tether the darksoul pulled taut. He yanked it back.

The fastest way to get them out of here would be to open a portal. Unfortunately, that wasn't in the cards. If he did that and didn't head straight to the Underworld with the heart and darksoul, Sutekh would want to know why. Any explanation would have to include Amber, and he wasn't fond of that plan, not until he had more information.

On the other hand, if he acted like a good delivery boy

and headed to the Underworld, he'd have to leave Amber behind. He couldn't leave her alone.

No. That was a lie. If nothing else, he ought to at least be honest with himself. He didn't *want* to leave her alone, didn't want Asmodeus's men to grab her, didn't want to lose her when he'd only just found her again.

Even after everything she'd done to him, he didn't want to just leave her behind. Talk about a twisted tangle of emotions. He hadn't been this turned around in decades, not since he'd gotten back from the heat and blood and death overseas.

He caught her cutting a look at the darksoul through her lashes. "Turn," he ordered, and together they rounded the elevators.

She skidded to a stop as they reached the far side.

"That's a—"

"Mint-condition 1960 Corvette convertible," he finished for her. White with red interior. Whitewall tires. Every nut and bolt original. Matching numbers, matching tags. It was the car he'd dreamed about buying way back in the day. How many nights had they sat beneath the stars and planned road trips in their imaginary Corvette? They were going to drive down the coast, then head to Arizona. Maybe even drive all the way across the country to New York City. She always said it didn't matter where they went, so long as they were together.

He remembered the birthday card she'd given him. Hand-made, with a picture of a corvette that she'd cut out of a magazine, the two of them drawn in to occupy the seats. The likenesses had been spot on. She'd always been an artist, always turning a coffee stain on a napkin into a fat bird with a few strokes of her pen or a chocolate smudge into a woman dancing in the rain. For a second he wondered if she still painted, still drew. He hadn't seen any pictures on her walls, and he suddenly realized that her art had never been lasting or permanent. Always something that could be tossed or disappear.

"The soul reaper business must be good," Amber said softly, a wistful edge in her words. And that made him remember just how broke they'd been once upon a time. Broke and happy.

He pulled open the passenger door and nudged her inside. As she looked up at him, he met her gaze.

"Yeah, business is good." He offered a smile that was all teeth and no warmth. "I kill people, Amber. Rip their hearts out. Steal their darksouls. Deliver them as a meal of pure power to the Underworld god who owns me."

He tossed the pouch with the heart onto the floor at her feet, but his eyes never left hers. He wanted to shock her, scare her, maybe even guilt her. He wanted her to hurt like he'd hurt. Like he still hurt.

"And sometimes," he continued, "if the dead have no heirs, then I help myself to what was theirs." He leaned in and she gasped, raising her hands to press her palms against his chest and hold him off. Then she flushed when all he did was drag the seat belt across her lap. He smiled at that. "I'm very good at what I do." He paused, letting that sink in. "And the pay's great."

All true. But he didn't say a word about the fact that he was low man on the totem pole and his existence was only assured if he could maintain his kill numbers. He survived on the edge. And somewhere along the way, he'd grown to like that, like the hunt, the kill. All of it.

He didn't hate his life, or rather, afterlife. In fact, he liked it just fine.

Amber was right. He wasn't her Kai. He wasn't the man

she'd known. That man, despite what he'd seen and done fighting for his country, had been little more than a boy. Fifty years as a reaper for the lord of chaos had changed that boy into something else entirely.

Kai's head kicked up as he heard the sound of a powerful engine and the squeal of tires. "Time to move."

He slammed the door shut, rounded the hood, slid into his seat, and got the car moving.

They reached the spiral exit ramp just as an enormous black Hummer bore down on them.

3

———

Amber dug her fingers into her thighs as Kai careered down the spiral ramp. They were going so fast she didn't know how he wasn't losing control of the car and scraping the wall.

"You can relax," he said. "I won't crash."

That wasn't what she was afraid of. If she died a fourth time, she'd just wake up hours later in the morgue, fully healed. She knew that from experience; her third death had been in a car crash.

She was afraid of the hunters, of what they would do once they caught her. She'd spent her entire life afraid of them. Her mother had sung that fear into her head like a lullaby, and the fact that they always managed to find her eventually and send her running all over again only strengthened it.

She twisted to look back. The Hummer was losing ground, and the driver's side scraped the concrete wall with a shriek and a shower of sparks.

Kai gave her a measured look. "Ready to tell me what they want with you?"

"I don't know."

"You lie so well I almost believe you. That's a talent," he said as they sped around the corner and onto Mission. Kai let the engine roar, and the car flew along the street. Then he cut a sharp right onto 10th.

Again, she looked behind them. The Hummer was back there, not gaining, but not losing ground, either.

"Why do you call them hunters?" he asked.

"Because they hunt me," she said, eyeing the greasy, black cloud that bobbed just behind Kai's head.

The look he shot her was glacial.

"Why?"

She shook her head. "I don't know."

"You keep singing that same song, and it doesn't get better with repetition." Kai took a corner so fast she was certain they were going to fly off the road and slam into the storefront. She held her breath, only releasing it when another look over her shoulder revealed that the Hummer was nowhere in sight.

That should have eased her mind. Instead, it made her edgy. "Too easy," she muttered.

"Yeah. They'll be back."

His left hand was relaxed on the wheel as they merged onto the I-80 east. His right hand rested on the knob of the gearshift. There was dried blood on his fingers. Long, strong fingers with blunt tips.

She looked away, not wanting to remember.

"Okay. Let's try a different question. How long have they been after you?" he asked.

She pressed her lips together. She didn't trust him. But he seemed to have a whole bucket load of information that she lacked. So, she was open to a little conversation.

She opened her mouth, then froze, the enormity of this

moment slamming her. For the first time since her mother's death, she could tell someone the truth. She could talk about the hunters, the fear, the fact that she was human, but not. She could tell Kai everything that she hadn't dared say when they were together all those years ago.

Whatever he was now, he'd been human then. If she'd told him the truth he'd have thought she was delusional. But he wasn't human now. Not anymore. And he had answers. He knew about things she'd never imagined.

"Who is Asmodeus?" she asked.

"Told you. Demon of lust."

"What does he want with me?"

Kai passed two cars, then tucked in front of a truck.

"If they're behind us, this'll offer a bit of cover," he said. Then he shrugged. "How am I supposed to know what Asmodeus wants with you? You made some deal with him or he wouldn't be hunting you. I just have to wonder what kind of deal. He's expending a shitload of manpower. Whatever you owe him, it's big, and he wants it."

"I don't owe him anything." Or did she? Was it possible that her mother had made a deal, that she'd inherited her mother's debt? The possibility chilled her.

"He was looking for you even then, when we were together, wasn't he?" Kai shot her an assessing look. "That's a lot of years to chase after someone who doesn't owe him anything, don't you think?"

"If I owe him something, I have no idea what it is." She paused. "He's been hunting me forever."

Kai kept his eyes on the road. "How long is forever?"

His tone was softer than it had been, luring her to trust him. As if.

"Since the day I was born," she said because there was no harm in offering that truth.

"Which was? You never did tell me. Never told me what day you were born. Or what year. And anything personal you did share was always vague, hazy. You said you grew up in Europe but never told me the name of the town or even the country."

"We moved a lot."

"You told me your mother died, but maybe she isn't dead at all. Maybe she's like you and somewhere out there is a first-generation Amber—"

"She's dead. She died. She closed her eyes one night and never opened them in the morning." She still missed her mother's smile, her laugh, the sound of her voice, even after all these years. "Her heart just stopped between one beat and the next."

Kai must have heard the pain in her voice because he conceded, "Okay. I'll accept that as truth. But I'm betting the rest was all lies." He stared straight ahead at the road, jaw tense. "Not that there was much you actually told me. You were the queen of evasion."

There was a thread of pain in his words. It stunned her. And shamed her. Because she *had* lied to him, again and again. Outright lies. Lies of evasion. Lies of omission.

"I'm going to ask a question now, an easy one, and I want the truth, Amber. One truth." Kai paused. "When were you born?"

"Just over a hundred years ago," she said, giving him that because a conversation couldn't happen with only one person doing the talking. And because it felt so good to tell the truth—even if it was just a small truth—at last.

"So when we were together..."

"I stopped aging at twenty-five. Maybe even before that, but when I was twenty-five I noticed my skin hadn't changed in a long time. Years. Not even a freckle or a faint line. Nothing."

Kai checked the mirrors but didn't appear concerned by what he saw. Still, she couldn't resist the need to check for herself. The Hummer was nowhere in sight.

"How do you know Asmodeus has been hunting you since you were born?"

How much to tell? How much was too much?

"We were always on the move, my mother and I. We never stayed in one place long. I don't remember a lot about my earliest years. I remember a village with a well and cobbled streets. There were hills all around. Very green. I remember cows and sheep and an old woman with a cane who gave me sweets that tasted of almonds. We left when I was five or so..." She turned her head and watched the scenery blur past.

"What happened when you were five?"

She swallowed. "We ran. We left everything behind."

"Because the hunters came?"

"No."

He didn't say anything as if he sensed this moment was fragile, that if he pushed he would get nothing.

Finally, she said, "Because I died. I died for the first time. I died and while the women of the village kept a vigil with my mother, I woke up." Once those words were out, more words came, and she found herself telling him all, hesitantly, then more easily, pausing every few sentences to check the side mirror or turn to look out the back window. The halting words became a steady flow and then a torrent. She told him everything. About her mother. The hunters. The terror that if they caught her they would do things to her that were worse than death.

She told him about sitting up and setting the village

women screaming, about fleeing so she and her mother wouldn't be bound to a stake and burned. She told him about opening her eyes in a cold room on a cold table in the morgue after her second death, draped in a sheet, surrounded by corpses. The horror of that had never faded.

She told him about watching her mother grow older and older and knowing that with her death, there would be no one left that she could trust, no one left who knew the truth. She told him about the terror and horror of knowing she would outlive everyone she might ever love, that she could never promise forever because it was a word that had a far different meaning for her.

She told him about her third death.

She told him not because she trusted him, but because she wanted him to trust her. To tell her what he knew.

And because it had been so long since she'd dared to utter such truths.

They left San Francisco far behind by the time she was done her story, and Kai never interrupted.

When she was done and fell silent, he said, "You should have told me this—"

"Really?" she cut him off before he could finish. "I should have told you this when we were together? You would have believed me? I don't think so. You would have thought I was on drugs or that I was insane."

He was silent long enough that she knew he conceded the point.

A flicker of movement caught her eye in the side mirror, and she spun to look through the back window. In the distance was the gleam of headlights coming in fast. There were no other cars on this stretch of highway now.

Kai eased up on the accelerator, letting their speed drop.

"What are you doing?" she asked. "We need to outrun them."

"Where's the challenge in that?"

"Challenge? You think this is a game?"

"Everything in life is a game, Amber. It's all about how much enjoyment you take from the play."

She was silent for an instant. The Kai she'd loved wouldn't have felt that way. He'd been solemn and serious, as solid as granite. He hadn't been one to take chances. He'd planned. He'd worked. He'd saved. It was one of the reasons she'd taken such pleasure in doing quirky things that surprised him and made him smile. He'd been serious and earnest and responsible. He'd been haunted by things he'd done, things he rarely spoke of. He'd been set on being a good man, creating a good life. She'd loved that solidity, that calm in the center of the storm that was her life.

So, what did it say about her that she found this new adventurous facet of his personality appealing? That she found just being with him, talking to him, catching him looking at her while she looked at him appealing?

He wasn't her Kai. He was someone else, honed and hard, and he was handsome as sin. But somewhere inside was the Kai she'd known. He still listened the same way, patient, glancing at her as he drove, nodding or making that humming sound to encourage her to keep going. He drove the same way. He still kept his nails neatly trimmed, his clothes in perfect repair. Little things that hadn't changed.

She looked away, wondering how she could be thinking those things while the hunters roared close behind them. What did she imagine? That Kai would keep her safe? She huffed a short laugh.

"Something funny?" he asked.

"No. Not at all. Not in the slightest." The truth. None of

this was funny. Especially not the hunters bearing down on them. "I was just thinking that you've left me without a weapon," she said. "What am I supposed to do? Rely on you to keep me safe?"

He laughed, the sound easy and unfettered, reaching deep inside her and twisting her in knots. Because that was Kai's laugh, and the memory of that laugh had been with her all these years.

"It's been forever since I kept anyone safe. This should be fun." He glanced at her, his dark eyes gleaming. Then he took pity on her and dipped his chin toward the glove box. "There's a knife in there if it'll make you feel better."

She popped the compartment open and snagged the knife. It was old, with an elaborately engraved handle and a curved blade. But at least it was a weapon. She closed her eyes for a second, remembering Kai's hands on hers as he showed her how to hold a knife, how to thrust. Forward grip. Reverse grip. *Don't extend your knife arm all the way. That leaves it vulnerable to attack, my little love.* "Yes, it makes me feel better, but I'd have preferred my gun."

"Some things don't change. You were never fond of knives."

"I was never really fond of guns, either. Evil necessity." She watched the side mirror and the approaching lights, heart pounding, mouth dry. "I'm sorry I shot you. I thought you were a hunter."

He grunted.

"It didn't even slow you down."

"Think of me as the improved version," Kai said. "It'd take more than a bullet to stop me." He cut her a glance. "But it still hurt like a bitch."

The Hummer roared up behind them, inches from the

rear bumper. There were no other cars in sight and all around them were fields. Endless fields.

"If they scratch my bumper, I'll kill them," Kai muttered, speeding up just enough to stay ahead of them.

Amber swallowed. Fear made her hands shake and sweat slick her spine as her blood rushed loud in her ears. "Don't you plan to kill them anyway?"

Kai grinned but said nothing.

The Hummer bumped them hard enough to make Amber's head rock. Kai's grin disappeared.

Yanking the wheel, Kai jerked the car to one side. Amber's shoulder hit the door. The lights from the Hummer disappeared from the mirror for a second then cut through the darkness once more as the driver aligned his course to Kai's.

"You think holding that's such a good idea?" he asked, gesturing at the knife. "At the rate we're going, you could stab yourself."

He spun the wheel and they veered sharply to the right, sending Amber sliding in the opposite direction along the seat. Again, the Hummer bumped them, harder this time.

Deciding he had a point, she popped the glove box, threw the knife back inside and slammed it shut just as the Hummer rammed them hard. There was a dull thud from under her feet and she looked down to see that the heart had rolled free of the leather pouch.

"Fuck," Kai snarled. "Can you pick that up for me?"

"What?"

The Hummer rammed them again. Amber grabbed the seat to balance herself against the blows. The heart rolled under her seat.

"Pick it up. Please," Kai said, his words painfully polite.

"I can't bring the darksoul without the heart and it's best if the heart doesn't look like ground meat when it gets there."

Amber started to lean down when the Hummer hit them again. Metal linked with metal and when Kai veered to the side, he didn't pull free.

"We're caught on their bumper," Amber said, pressing her open palm against the door as they swerved side to side.

"No shit. The repairs are going to cost a fucking fortune. If I didn't plan to kill them already, this would seal the deal."

Kai hit the brakes. Tires squealed. Amber smelled something burning. Brakes. Or tires. Maybe both.

The Hummer kept going, lifting and rolling forward, crushing the back of the Corvette. Amber unhitched her seatbelt and grabbed the door handle, ready to run. Her heart raced, her breathing too fast. The Hummer stopped where the hardtop started, inches short of crushing her and Kai.

"You okay?" he asked.

"No." She popped the glove box and retrieved the knife.

He threw open his door and got out, leaving the darksoul behind, his expression thunderous. Only after he was gone did she wonder at the concern she'd read in his eyes.

She glanced down to find the heart resting against her heel. She grabbed it, and as an afterthought reached for the bright band that tethered the darksoul, dragging it behind her as she left the car. She hesitated for a split second, unsure which way to turn before she decided on distance. Eyes locked on the scene before her, she backed away.

Kai was talking to the hunters, hands spread, palms up, unarmed, though all of them had guns pointed at him. His tone was low, and she heard only snippets of what he said— her name, then, "Toronto," and finally, "Asmodeus" and "non-negotiable."

What the hell had she been thinking, trusting Kai? He could be selling her out right now, making a deal to hand her over to the hunters.

Terror surged, leaving her breathless.

She looked around, frantic, her thoughts focused only on escape. Run. Hide. Endless fields stretched on all sides. There was nowhere to run. Nowhere to hide.

The hunters' voices rose, angry, aggressive. Amber spun back toward the hunters and Kai. Shots rang out.

Kai twitched as they shot him. Amber felt sick, her heart pounding, horror suffusing her. *Kai.*

He hadn't sold her out. He'd been arguing to keep her safe.

She cried out, not because of what his death meant in terms of her safety, but because she felt each shot like an arrow to her soul. She couldn't stand it if he died, couldn't bear it if she were the cause.

With a yell, she flipped the knife into throwing position and let it soar. Her aim was true. The blade pierced the nearest hunter's throat and remained there, the hilt vibrating. The man's hands came up, clawing, grasping. Too late.

Still standing, despite his wounds, Kai shot her a look and grinned. Then he turned back to the remaining men, his smile feral now, white teeth and the promise of death, and when he moved, she barely saw him. All she saw was the surprise etched on the hunters' faces as he killed them, one by one, ripping free their hearts.

"I told you to walk away but you wouldn't fucking listen," he snarled, going after the last hunter, who backed away, features twisted in terror. "I told you to just let her go and leave. I gave you the choice and you didn't choose wisely."

When it was done, Kai stood there, breathing hard,

blood covering his hands and forearms, a spray of it marking his face. And all around him, like fallen dominoes, the bodies of the dead.

He turned and his gaze raked her. "Nice aim." Then he strode toward her, eyes glittering, mouth hard. He stopped a foot away, and she could feel energy pounding off him in waves.

"You killed them," she said.

"Yeah."

"Because they scratched your bumper?"

He frowned, and she realized he was thinking back, trying to figure out why she asked that. Then his brows rose and she knew he'd remembered his earlier comment.

"No," he said and shot a glance at the darksoul, then the bright band that held it, following the thin thread down to her hand. He stared at her hand for a long time. Too long. "Because I didn't want them to put a scratch on you."

She gasped.

"And from the way you threw that knife, I'm guessing you weren't too keen on having them put a scratch on me," he said. He stepped closer and grabbed her wrist, unmindful of the blood that slicked his hands. He dragged her against him, hard muscle and heat. Lowering his mouth, he kissed her, his lips opening on hers, his tongue sliding inside.

And, heaven help her, she let him.

No, she didn't just let him. She dug her fingers into the solid muscle of his shoulders, held him close and kissed him back.

4

———

KAI WATCHED AMBER AS HE PULLED OUT HIS PHONE, LET HIS finger hover for a second before he chose a number and hit speed dial. Her shoulders were tense and she refused to look at him. She hadn't looked at him since she'd broken the kiss and stepped away. But she was still holding the tether of pure energy tied to the darksoul Kai had harvested earlier. He wouldn't have believed that if he weren't seeing it with his own eyes because as far as he knew, only soul reapers and Underworld gods and demons could grab hold of that kind of power.

All soul reapers were male; hence, Amber wasn't a soul reaper.

All Underworld gods couldn't leave the Underworld; hence, she wasn't one of them.

The only demons powerful enough to touch the band of fire were Asmodeus, Xaphan, Astaroth, Damballa, Cimeries, and Azazel. None of them could leave the Underworld, and none of them were Amber.

So, what the fucking hell was she? He had a feeling that

if he could just answer that question, he'd know why Asmodeus was hunting her.

"I need cleanup," he said when Mal answered.

Mal laughed. "Again? That's twice in one night. You've been busy."

"You could say that."

When he finished giving Mal the details of their location, Kai shoved his phone back in his pocket and approached Amber, stopping a couple of feet away when she spun toward him, eyes wide and wary.

The way he saw it, he had two choices. Talk to her about that kiss. Or not. He went with not. For the moment, at least. She was strung so tight he thought the slightest breath of wind might make her snap like an overstretched elastic band.

"I'll take that," he said, reaching for the darksoul and the pouch that held the heart.

Her gaze slid to the bodies that littered the road. They'd been lucky that no other cars had come along. It might be a bit difficult to explain away the carnage.

"Why didn't you do the same thing to them? Take their darksouls and keep their hearts?" she asked. "You ripped them out and then left them there."

Kai measured his response and pared it down to the bare bones of the truth.

"The Underworld's divided up into Territories, sort of like crime syndicates divide up cities, I guess. All the gods and demigods hold sway in their own kingdoms. And they have Topworld grunts—"

"Like them." She looked at the bodies again.

"Like them," he agreed. "The gods run rackets Topworld. Drugs. Women. Real-estate fraud. Weapons. Anything that makes money to fund their Topworld pursuits. But money isn't the true goal. They're all after the souls. That's the currency that matters in the Underworld, and the Topworld rackets are just a way to get them. But there's sort of an unwritten rule that we don't recklessly harvest from another lord's crew."

"But you killed them. All of them."

He rubbed the back of his neck. "They were a threat." *To you.*

"So it's okay that you killed them?"

"Guess that depends on your definition of okay. It won't start a war if that's what you're asking."

She waved a hand at the darksoul bobbing above them. "You took *his* darksoul."

She was completely calm, her expression perfectly neutral. He couldn't decide if that was because she was a breath away from freaking out or because she was numb with shock. He studied her for a second and amended his thoughts. Maybe it was because she was a woman who couldn't die, who'd spent a lifetime thinking she was the only one of her kind, who'd spent that same lifetime evading an unspecified, shadowy threat. Maybe she just wanted knowledge because she'd spent a lifetime flying blind.

Amber was tough. She'd had to be.

He jutted his chin toward the darksoul. "He had a prior debt to Sutekh. I was sent to harvest him."

"And to find out why Asmodeus sent men to San Francisco," Amber added.

"That, too," Kai agreed.

For a while there, he'd thought he'd only accomplish one of the two. But now he was certain of Asmodeus's motives; he wanted Amber. Problem was, that knowledge put Kai in a damn tight spot—he didn't want to share that information with Sutekh because that would make Amber far too interesting to the Lord of Chaos.

They both stared at the mangled corpses. "Sorry," he said.

"Don't be. What did you think I meant to do with the gun you crushed?" She held his gaze. "I was going to kill them to make certain they could never come after me again. And I used your knife to kill one so he couldn't go after you." She paused. "Or are you sorry for kissing me?"

"Not sorry for that." Kai rubbed his palm over the back of his neck. "Are you? Cause you were definitely kissing me back."

Her gaze slid to the Corvette, squashed like a bug beneath the weight of the Hummer. He winced just to look at it.

"They didn't try to kill you," he said. "You were shot in the shoulder, not head or heart. They didn't aim for you when you got out of the car. They didn't crush the hard-top when that would have been a pretty surefire way to kill you. It makes no sense. If you owe Asmodeus, then your death would take your soul straight to him. Why not kill you?"

"I can't die," she said.

Kai pinned her with a look. "Did they know that?"

She frowned, opened her mouth, then shut it again. "What now?" she asked, her voice subdued.

It was a loaded question, and telling her the answers all at once might not be the best plan. Instead, he asked a question of his own because he'd heard her cry out when the grunts had shot him, she'd killed a man so that man wouldn't harm him, and he'd tasted the welcome in her kiss. None of which pointed to a woman who wanted him dead.

"The night I was killed, why did you send me to Pfeiffer Beach?"

"I didn't send you anywhere."

He let that pass for the moment. "I looked for you," he said, revealing more than he meant to. "Time passes differently in the Underworld. Once I could leave, months had gone by. I tried to find you. Everything was gone. Your clothes. Your toothbrush. There wasn't a thread or button or pin to show that you'd ever been there. I might have thought I'd imagined all those months we were together—"

"I left nothing that could lead them to me."

"Why did you send me to Pfeiffer Beach?"

"I didn't."

Damn, she had that look down pat, the one where she met and held his gaze, even, controlled. "It was your lipstick on the mirror. Your handwriting."

"There was no note on the mirror. I didn't write one and it wasn't there when I went back..." Her voice trailed away and she frowned.

"What?" he asked.

She shook her head. "Nothing."

"Something. Tell me."

"The mirror. It was smudgy. All these years later, I remember because that was so odd. You were a clean freak. You made your bed every morning, so tight I could bounce a quarter off it. You never left dishes in the kitchen sink. Your mirrors were never smudgy. The one time you let your car get dirty—"

"You drew a heart around our initials."

She huffed a soft laugh. "We acted like children."

"We were happy," Kai said, the words ringing true in his heart. They'd been happy. So why send him to die?

For a long moment she only stared at him, and then she whispered, "You sent me to Coit Tower."

"I didn't." Now he was the one to hold her gaze, willing her to see the truth of his words. "What happened at Coit Tower?"

"You lured me there. You sent me roses. And a note. 'Coit Tower at midnight.'"

"Roses." He stilled, feeling betrayed all over again. He tamped down that emotion, realizing it was ridiculous, but unable to completely ignore it. Had she not known him at all? *Roses.* "All these years, you thought I lured you to Coit Tower with fucking *roses*? What happened there?"

"You know what happened. The hunters were waiting for me. I barely escaped."

"But you did escape. How?"

"They didn't use lethal force." Her gaze slid back to the crushed Corvette. His followed.

They wanted Amber alive.

Why?

"And you think I sent you into a trap?" Everything about this felt wrong.

"You think I sent you to Pfeiffer Beach," she shot back.

Check. Mate. She snared him in a world of pale brown and gold and all he saw were her eyes and years of hurt layered on hurt.

"No," he said in all honesty, forcing himself to step beyond habit, beyond the dark certainties and black anger that had haunted him for decades. "Not anymore. I think someone else lured me there using you as bait. And I think someone used me as bait to get you to Coit Tower. They wanted me dead. And they wanted you alive."

She stared at him, her chest rising and falling too fast.

"I wouldn't have sent you roses," he said at last. "I'd have sent you daisies. Gerberas. You should have fucking known that, Amber. You didn't even like roses."

"I didn't. Still don't."

He reached for her, then froze and drew back as the air beside them shimmered and changed. Electricity danced across his skin, and he knew Amber felt it too because she jerked and rubbed her palms along her forearms. Dark, undulating smog appeared before them, pulling in on itself before bursting outward.

A man stepped through the black mist. His hair was dark, his eyes pale gray. He wore two hoops in each ear, a day's worth of stubble, and a dangerous grin.

"Mal," Kai greeted him and tossed him the keys to the Corvette. "I appreciate this."

Mal caught the keys and shot a curious look at Amber. But he didn't ask. "I'll call you next time I need cleanup," was all he said.

"Can you make the delivery for me, as well?" Kai jerked the darksoul forward.

"And count the kill as mine?"

"No. But I'll owe you a delivery, as well as a cleanup."

"Done," Mal said, flicking another glance in Amber's direction.

She studied him with interest and he waggled his brows. Classic Mal.

"Don't even think it," Kai said, offering no explanation. This wasn't Mal's business. And Amber wasn't Mal's type— all fun, no strings.

Amber wasn't anyone's type, but his.

He handed off the darksoul and the heart, then turned to Amber and said, "Let's go."

"Go? The car isn't drivable."

He winced at the reminder. That car was his baby. "It

can be fixed. For now, the Hummer will get us where we need to go."

It wasn't until they were in the vehicle and pulling away that she asked, "And where is it that we need to go?"

He could see she wasn't pleased when he didn't offer an answer. Not that he was being evasive. He just didn't know how to tell her that he had a suspicion about why Asmodeus had spent a hundred years looking for her. A hunch. All he'd needed to do was turn the puzzle pieces upside down and look at them a whole new way.

Once he looked for the unexpected, for motives that were other than they first appeared, everything slid into place.

They pieces fit perfectly now.

But he didn't think Amber was going to like the end product they formed.

"Where are we?" Amber stirred in the seat and pushed her hair back out of her face. They'd been driving for about twenty hours, alone in the Hummer, stopping only at gas stations.

They'd talked about a thousand things, none of them important.

Little things. The changes they'd seen in the world. New technologies and inventions. Places they'd been. She'd walked on the Great Wall of China. He'd been diving on the Great Barrier Reef.

He almost found himself promising to take her there.

But they didn't touch on anything personal. Anytime either of them even prodded at the edges of personal, they both went silent. And every time they went silent, Kai thought of the kiss.

"We're coming up on Cheyenne," he said, pulling into the lot of the Central Motel, which actually wasn't central at all. "Wait here. I'll get a room."

He waited a beat for her to tell him to get two rooms, or at least, two beds, but she said nothing, only cut him a quiet look from beneath her lashes.

Then she looked out the window and said, "It's raining."

It was. In buckets.

"It was raining the day we met."

"Yeah." He stared at the windshield wipers as they whumped back and forth, thinking how long ago that day had been. Less than a memory. Almost a dream.

Heading into the motel office, he paid cash and got a key. There was a small selection of toiletries and snacks, so he picked up a couple of toothbrushes, toothpaste, shampoo, soap. Then he headed back to the Hummer and drove them around to their room. It was an end unit, as he'd requested, and it opened to the back parking lot rather than the road.

There wasn't another car in sight back here, though there had been two or three parked out front.

He pulled into a spot, got out, rounded to Amber's door. He was drenched by the time he got there, the rain pouring down on him.

He yanked the door open. "Run for it—"

"No," she said, rested her hands on his shoulders and slid from her seat, her body contacting his all the way down.

The rain streamed over them both, leaving her shirt molded to her body and her hair hanging in wet trails.

That fast, lust roared. That fast, emotion swamped him.

He was glad she wasn't hurt. Glad she wasn't dead. Glad she was here. More than glad.

Slamming the door shut, he backed her against it. He let the plastic bag of toiletries drop to the ground, his hands coming up to cup her cheeks, to hold her still. He pinned her with his weight and lowered his mouth to hers. She opened with a sigh and tipped her face to his. It was all the invitation he needed. With a growl, he took the kiss deeper and felt a primitive satisfaction when she let him in.

He ran his hands along the curves of her waist, the soft swells of her breasts, a little rough, a lot uncouth. She didn't seem to mind, her hands cupping his ass and dragging him closer.

Need and want. Desire for her pounded him. He'd long ago washed the blood from his hands at the first service station they'd stopped at, and now the rain felt like it washed away all his anger, all the misconceptions he'd harbored. The past. The pain.

In this moment, there was only Amber, the scent of her skin and the smell of the rain. Her hair was wet, heavy silk in his hands. And under the cool sheets of rain, they made their own heat.

He moved his lips to her throat, tasting her, his teeth nipping, his tongue soothing the hurt. She closed her fists on the material of his shirt, her breath coming in short, sharp pants as she clung to him.

Then she spun him so it was his back against the Hummer and her weight pressed against his, her curves melding with his lines and angles as she came up on her toes and pressed herself against him.

She ran her hands over his chest, his abdomen, lower.

His dick was so hard it hurt. He caught her wrists and held fast as she tried to tug free.

He wanted to kiss her, worship her, celebrate the impossible gift of these hours with her. He wanted to pin her beneath him. He wanted to stroke and tease and play. He wanted to sink deep inside her and take them both to the edge a million times before letting them soar free.

Without a word, he scooped up the bag, then scooped her into his arms. Holding her against his chest, he strode to the room and unlocked the door.

5

———

Kai tossed the bag of toiletries on the dresser as he kicked the door shut behind him.

He set Amber on her feet, his mouth on hers, tongues dancing, heat roaring through him. He grabbed the hem of her shirt. The wet material fought his every move as he dragged it up, over her head, her arms trapped in wet cloth. The delay was torture, and pleasure, slowing everything down so he savored every breath she took, every gasp, every sigh.

He pressed his lips to the soft skin where her neck met her shoulder. And then finally the shirt was gone and she stood before him, naked from the waist up except for a black lacy bra. He didn't take it off. Only pushed the cups down, leaving her breasts bare and pushed high in luscious invitation.

Her breath hitched and she lifted her chin.

"You are the most gorgeous woman I've ever seen," Kai said.

He'd said those exact words to her the first time he'd peeled her clothes from her body. The look on her face told him she remembered. He'd meant them then. He meant them now.

He kissed her neck, her collarbone, the hollow at the base of her throat, his thumb brushing the tip of her breast. She gasped and arched against him as he lowered his head and sucked her nipple to a sweet, taut peak, then did the same with the other, leaving them both pink and wet.

"Kai," she whispered, her hands flat against his chest. Permission or protest, for a second he couldn't be sure.

Then she pushed at his shirt, the sodden material stubborn against her efforts, and he had his answer. In the end, he struggled out of his clothes as she worked her wet jeans down the length of her legs, both of them huffing and laughing. It didn't lessen his hard-on.

"Well worth the effort," he said when at last they were both naked. He paused for an instant, looking his fill. She stood on one foot, the other still trapped in wet denim, one hand resting on the bed for balance as she leaned forward at the waist.

A thin stream of light from the single lamp that illuminated the parking lot filtered through the narrow slit in the curtains. It was enough to paint her in shades of glitter and gold.

He'd been waiting for her for decades, dreaming of her for eternity, the memories teasing him until they caused him physical pain. He'd been aching for a woman he thought he'd never see again. And now she was here. She was warm and willing, her skin silky and still damp, her eyes heavy lidded as she watched him.

She was perfect.

He was on fire; he was so hard he thought the slightest touch would make him burst.

Catching her around the waist, he tumbled with her to the bed.

He was too rough as he pushed her legs apart. He knew that, but she didn't seem to care. Her arms wrapped around his shoulders as she pressed her mouth to his, her lips open, her tongue seeking. She tasted him as he tasted her, deep, wet.

Her legs came around his hips, her mons brushing the head of his erection.

Reaching between them, he stroked her soft folds, found her wet, ready. With a low growl, he pushed two fingers inside her, without finesse or tact, the heel of his palm pressing against her swollen clit. She welcomed him, her hips arching against his hand. She was slick and hot and so damned tight.

"Kai, now," she breathed, words so soft they were almost without sound.

She was supple beneath him, warm and welcoming. He slid his fingers from her heat, letting them glide over the swollen nub of her clit, dragging a low moan from her.

Then he shifted and pressed the head of his dick against her opening, easing in just a little. She was so damn tight. Hot. Wet. He thrust inside, her muscles easing as she opened to the invasion. A coil of raw pleasure made him groan.

She angled her hips and made a sound somewhere between a groan and a purr, her eyes wide open as she studied his face.

It was like she could see past his skin and muscle, past his shell to what lay at his core. He wasn't sure he wanted her to see more than skin deep.

He shifted his hips and gave a swift pump, in, out. Her lids drifted shut and she gave a hum of approval.

He hooked her knee, brought it higher, opening her still more, and she sucked in a breath as he pushed fully inside her, feeling her close around him, tight and lush.

He pulled back and gave a shallow thrust and another, until she dug her nails into his buttocks and ordered, "More."

Taking his thrusts deeper, harder, he made her gasp, made her moan, slowing each time she moved to match his pace, to take them both closer to the edge.

"Bastard," she whispered without heat.

"Kai," he whispered back and kissed her. "My name is Kai and you'll scream it when I make you come."

"Make me come now and I'll scream as loud as you want."

He caught her wrists and dragged them above her head. "Patience is a virtue," he said and laughed when she reared up and bit him.

***

He overwhelmed her. He ruled her. And she let him, the pleasure coming over her in waves. Amber rode each one higher, closer to the edge.

Rising up on his outstretched arms, Kai watched her face as he took her, and she watched his. He was beautiful. Primitive. Hard muscle under smooth dark skin. He was everything she had ever wanted, ever dreamed of.

The fringe of wet, spiky lashes cast shadows on his cheeks. His eyes were so dark they looked black in this light, beautiful, deep, glittering with something she was afraid to acknowledge. Something that found its match in her heart.

She felt the heat and the power of him as he moved

inside her, setting the rhythm they both followed, carrying her higher and higher, but never high enough.

"Kai, please."

Lowering his head, he drew on her nipple, a languid tug that turned into something more. A sharper suction, then the gentle stroke of his tongue that sent pleasure streaking through her veins.

Her eyes flew open, and she gasped as he scraped his teeth along the sensitive flesh, then licked her before using his teeth once more. It was pain. It was pleasure. She clung to him, moving as he moved, meeting each thrust, hungry and wild.

He reared back, his expression savage, his hips moving in perfect rhythm. With a moan, she gave herself over to him, to the rhythm and the pleasure of his thrusts as he drove into her in rough, hard strokes that made her entire body sing.

A raw sound tore from deep in his throat, hard-edged need and animal lust, and he moved in long, full strokes, harder, faster.

"Kai," she whimpered, then screamed, "Kai," as she unraveled, her body clenched tight around him. He swallowed the sound with his kiss.

Ecstasy rode her senses, blurring her thoughts as her orgasm rocked her, going on and on.

He rode her through her release and then she felt his whole body go tense, felt him shudder against her, his orgasm tearing through him.

She was lost and found and so happy in that moment. The world was hers and perfection was real.

Panting, Kai dropped his head, nuzzling the curve of her neck. She felt liquid and light, as though she were floating. At the same time, she felt wonderfully, incredibly alive.

She closed her eyes and lay beneath him, loving the weight of his body on hers. She thought she might have dozed, though she had no idea for how long. Drowsy, replete, she lay there, only slowly becoming aware that he was moving, kissing his way down her body, teasing her to life, taking his time as he rekindled her desire.

"Some things haven't changed," she murmured, tangling her fingers in his hair. When they'd been together, he'd always liked to make love more than once.

Make love. Was that what they were doing here?

This man who had just turned her boneless, who was kissing and nipping his way along her body and bringing it to life once more wasn't the man he had been. He was different. He'd changed. And she hadn't been there to see those changes.

They were different people. New people. Yet still the same somehow. She wasn't sure exactly what to call the emotions that bubbled through her.

She felt something for him, something that wasn't just attraction, was it? Her heart tripped a stuttering rhythm before she forced those thoughts to the back of her mind. She couldn't think about that, about love or what they'd had or what they'd lost. She could only let herself think about now. And as Kai found her clit and stroked his tongue along the sensitized bud, she let her head fall back and she thought about nothing at all.

He took her again and again through the night, driving them both over the edge.

And finally, she slept, wrapped in the safety of his arms, the deepest sleep she'd had in decades.

WHEN AMBER WOKE, THE SUN WAS HIGH AND KAI WAS SITTING on the foot of the bed, fully dressed, holding a tray with two steaming cups of coffee.

Pushing upright, she held the sheet against her breasts.

"You don't think it's a bit late for modesty?" he asked, dark eyes narrowing.

"It is, isn't it?" So, she dropped the sheet.

With deliberate care, he set the coffees on the dresser. "They'll get cold," he warned.

"Then we'll drink them cold."

He rose and pulled his shirt over his head, baring his naked torso, lean and hard. Her pulse kicked up and she looked her fill.

"You're not too sore?" he asked.

"I heal fast."

He slid his fingers to his waist and took his time slipping the button free, pulling the zipper down.

Then he raised his gaze to hers and cocked a brow. "More?"

"Let me." She scooted forward and curled her fingers into the waistband of his jeans. His skin was warm, her fingers cool. She smiled as she felt his muscles jump beneath her touch.

Slowly she worked his jeans down his legs, taking the time to kiss his belly, the arc of his hip bone, the bulge of his erection through his boxers. She kissed his muscled thighs as she worked his jeans down to his ankles.

He kicked them free and was on her in a millisecond, his hands trailing fire, stirring her senses and her heart. He made love to her with his lips, with his hands, with his body.

In the end, she lay sprawled atop him, breathing raggedly, heart singing.

They drank cold coffee and ate Danishes so sweet they made her teeth hurt.

Then they showered together and dressed in clothes Kai had bought in town. Nothing fancy. Jeans and T-shirts. She was surprised at how well he'd judged her size. And she was glad not to have to put the clothes that had been drenched the night before back on. They were dry but stiff, and stained with blood.

"I want to take you to Toronto," he said when they were ready to leave.

Her heart gave a hard thump against her ribs. He wanted to take her straight into danger. He wanted to expose her to—

No. She wasn't going to do that. She wasn't going to let fear rule her. "Why?" she asked.

His jaw tensed. "I want to talk to a guy by the name of Big Ralph. I want to know why Asmodeus sent his crew after you."

"So you want to take me to the place that Asmodeus is strongest. Those men he sent to kill me came from there. You're taking me to them. To the hunters I've been running from my whole life."

"I can keep you safe," Kai said.

"Can you? How do you know? How can you be sure? You don't even know why they want me." She surged to her feet and paced across the room, feeling trapped and afraid. "When I was small, they were the monsters beneath my bed. And you want me to go right to them? Deliver myself like a gift?"

Hurt flashed across his features before he masked it.

"Do you think I'd let them take you? Hurt you?" he asked, his voice low and intense.

"Why should I trust you?" The words were out before

she could stop them, like a gun misfiring without the shooter's intent. The bullet flew free to do what damage it would, and it was too late to call it back, even if she wanted to.

Did she want to? Did she dare trust him?

She knew almost nothing about what he'd become and what exactly it meant to be a soul reaper. She didn't know if he lived in the same world she did, or if he spent most of his time in the Underworld. Were there limitations? Conditions? Could his loyalties to his master force him to turn on her?

Everything was so confused and confusing.

And lovemaking didn't equal love.

Had she ever stopped loving him?

Pain arrowed through her, sharp and bright. She'd never stopped. She'd loved him and hated him. She loved him still.

She met his gaze, wondering how much her expression gave away.

She thought he would turn away, perhaps become angry, but he only came to her slowly, as though approaching a wild thing that would bolt at being cornered.

"Amber," he whispered her name as he took her hand and drew her against him. "I'm not human anymore. There's only one way I can die now, and I have no intention of walking into the lakes of fire. My role as one of Sutekh's soul reapers protects me in ways I can't begin to explain."

"But it doesn't protect *me*. I noticed that you didn't explain me to that other soul reaper, Mal. Do you think I don't know why? The less he knows, the better, right?"

"I'm private by nature," Kai said.

"You always were." She closed her eyes, seeing the hunters as they came through the apartment door. Then she opened her eyes and looked at Kai. "I'm so tired of running. Of being alone."

"You're not alone anymore."

"Don't," she said, all her pain pouring into the word. "Don't you say that to me ever again. I have always been alone, the only one of my kind, always running, watching those I cared about age and die." She held up a hand, palm forward, when he made a move to come to her. "You once promised me forever and you didn't even know what it meant. Don't you tell me that I'm not alone."

"I *will* say it. It's the truth. You thought you were the only one of your kind, never dying, never aging, always healing. But you aren't. I may not be whatever the hell it is that you are, but I don't age. I don't die. I heal." He lifted his T-shirt and bared his chest, smooth skin over contoured muscle. There wasn't even a scar to mark the place where she'd shot him through the heart. "I may not know exactly what you are, but I do know you're a supernatural of some sort, and so am I. I will keep you safe."

"You can't," she whispered, blinking against the treacherous sting of tears. "You told me about your life, about how precarious your position is. You can't even guarantee your own safety."

His jaw tightened, but he didn't argue. Then he tried a different argument. "Fine. There are no real guarantees in anything. Not for humans and not for supernaturals. But I have this feeling that the hunters don't want to hurt you—"

"They've been after me my whole life—"

"And they've never used real force, right? I don't think they want to hurt you. I don't think they want to take you somewhere where you'll be hurt. I think they want you for a different reason."

"What reason?"

"That's why we need to confront Big Ralph. To find out." He paused. "You said you're sick of running. Well, you could stop. You could stay put. We could be together. We could face whatever comes at us together. We could work to keep each other safe."

His words reached inside and twisted her up because this wasn't a guarantee of safety. She would never be able to believe that as truth, and Kai knew that. Instead, he offered something that teased her, lured her, something she *could* believe. A chance. A possibility. Hope.

He took her hands and brought them to his lips. "I never stopped loving you, Amber, even when I believed you'd sent me to die. A part of me hated you, but a part of me never stopped loving you." He took a breath. "My last thought as I died was of you. My first thought when I got to the Underworld was of you."

His words mirrored the exact emotions of her heart. Even when she had believed he had betrayed her, a part of her had loved him with an eternal flame. "I..." She was afraid of the words, afraid that if she said them they would summon loss and pain. But she couldn't—wouldn't—live that way. "I never stopped loving you, Kai."

"I will die before I let anyone hurt you," he said. "I will die before I let anyone take you from me." He grinned, white teeth against full lips and dark stubble. "And since I can't die..."

He wrapped his arms around her and drew her close, his heart thudding a steady beat against her ear, and she realized that a part of her believed him, believed in his dream, believed that this time she would finally stop running.

And a part of her believed that she would be running forever and that Kai's commitment to the god who owned his soul would keep him from running with her.

6

—————

Toronto, Canada

Three days later

At the counter of the coffee shop, Kai tipped his head to one side and stood perfectly still, his hand half extended with a bill pinched between his thumb and forefinger. Amber collected their cappuccinos as the man behind the cash looked at him questioningly. But Kai's attention wasn't on the guy, it was on the shelf behind him, above the cash register.

Amber followed his gaze. He was staring at a small gray box that had what appeared to be hieroglyphics engraved on the lid and sides.

"Where did you get that?" Kai asked.

The man cast a look over his shoulder. "The ROM gift shop."

"ROM?" Amber asked.

"Royal Ontario Museum. They had this exhibit of the ancient Egyptian Book of the Dead." The guy frowned. "I think it's over now. Too bad. I wouldn't have minded seeing it again."

"The box?" Kai urged.

The guy at the cash gave a dismissive wave. "I bought it in the gift shop for my girlfriend. That's her." He jutted his chin toward the woman steaming milk. "It was just sitting there, one of a kind." He laughed. "Or maybe it was the last one they had or something. There wasn't even a price on it. But the cashier was going off shift and she seemed okay just sort of comparing it to some jewelry boxes that were about the same size and she charged me the same price and that was that."

"What do you keep inside?" Kai asked, and Amber wondered at his interest. Sutekh was an Egyptian deity, so maybe that was the connection.

"Nothing." Again, the guy glanced over his shoulder at the box, then turned back to face them. "It doesn't open. I think it's hollow because it isn't that heavy, but I've looked and looked and I really can't see a way to open it. There's no secret catch or anything."

"May I?" Kai asked, and held out his hand, palm up.

"Sure."

He passed Kai the box. It was about the size and shape of four paperback novels stacked up. This close, Amber got a strange vibe off of it, a prickling of electricity dancing through her body, the same sort she'd felt when Mal had arrived to clean up the bodies. Maybe it was some sort of supernatural radar.

Maybe the box was blessed, or cursed, or imbued with some sort of power. This was all so new to her, knowing that other supernatural beings existed, that she wasn't sure what to make of any of it.

Kai turned the box in his hands, his expression tight. His fingers danced over the markings, traced the edges and corners, and his frown deepened. Drawn to the strange vibe, Amber touched the side, cold metal, the shapes raised and smooth beneath her touch. She felt like a cold wind blew against the back of her neck. The fine hairs at her nape rose as she watched Kai turn the box upright once more, almost reverent in the way he handled it.

"I'd like to buy this from you," he said.

The woman at the steamer laughed and called out, "Not for sale. Sorry. I swear, it's our good-luck charm. Ever since he bought it, business here has been crazy good."

"You sure?" Kai asked. "Name a price."

The guy behind the cash looked interested, but the woman said, "Nope. He's bought me exactly one gift since we started dating three years ago. That box. I'm not giving it up."

Amber searched Kai's face as he set the box on the counter. He seemed perfectly fine to let the matter go as they took their coffees to a table by the window, but she sensed his preoccupation, and she wondered at it.

"Everything okay?" she asked.

"Yeah." He lifted his coffee and took a sip. "A-okay."

"Why so interested in a knickknack?"

"Just a feeling it might be of interest to Sutekh."

She arched a brow. "He collects knickknacks?"

Kai laughed. "Something like that." He tapped his fingers on the tabletop. Amber blew on her coffee and waited. Finally, Kai nodded toward the street. "We're going to head to Tesso's when we're done here," he said, then lowered his voice. "It's a bar around the corner, and it's run by Topworlders who run prostitutes for Asmodeus. There will be a *gentleman*—" a hint of sarcasm flavored the word "—there tonight who has a particular tie to Asmodeus. Big Ralph. I will not leave your side. I'll invoke Sutekh's protection to keep you safe. But I'm done with you having to run and hide. We're going to find out what the hell is going on once and for all." He paused and lifted his gaze to hers. "And then you'll be free."

Free. No more running. No more hunters.

She didn't even know what she'd do with her life, if she'd settle in one place or keep moving. She'd be a nomad for a century. Freedom to choose was something she'd never expected.

Kai must have read something in her expression because he reached across the table and slid his fingers between hers. She stared at their clasped hands, her hand tiny in his, and then she looked up to find him watching her with a wistful smile.

He would never be free.

From all he'd said, she understood that much. He was sworn to Sutekh for eternity.

"I'm not sure I want to do this, go to Tesso's, talk to Big Ralph," she said. But she knew it was time. Whether she liked it or not, it really was past time for her to confront her demons.

Kai scooted his chair closer and cupped his hand around the base of her skull, leaning forward to rest his forehead against hers. "Better this wa—"

"Hey," the woman manning the milk steamer yelled. "Hey, give that back!"

Amber turned to see a guy with long greasy hair and baggy jeans tear toward the door. In his hand was the box Kai had been so interested in. She realized that the guy at the cash must have left it on the counter where Kai placed it earlier, rather than moving it back to the shelf.

And now some guy was stealing it.

Already on his feet and halfway to the door, Kai hesitated and spun back and faced her.

"Go," she said. "I'm in a public place. And no one knows we're here. Go."

"Stay here," he said, his expression torn. He obviously hated to leave her almost as much as he hated to let that box go.

That box was not just some knickknack.

The guy from behind the cash had already run into the street.

The barista was still yelling, standing in the open door, obviously wanting to chase the thief down, but unwilling to leave the shop unattended.

"Go," Amber said again. "I'll be fine."

"Stay put," Kai said. Then he went.

THEY CAME FOR HER LESS THAN TEN MINUTES LATER. AMBER couldn't help but wonder about how the whole thing had played out; she wondered if the hunters had set up that greasy haired guy to lure Kai from her side.

Five men surrounded her. She had no weapon and little likelihood of making it past them and getting away. She waited for the panic to set in, the certainty that the hunters would take her to a fate worse than death itself.

There *was* fear, no doubt about that.

But it wasn't the panic that had always dogged her when she came close to the hunters. Her time spent with Kai had made her see things a little differently.

She couldn't die.

She knew a thing or two about self-defense.

And Kai would come for her.

They didn't offer a word of explanation, just flanked her on all sides as they led her from the coffee shop into the street. She said nothing, kept her head down, and plotted. There were two behind her, two in front and one on her right. The street was to her left. She waited until a car was almost abreast of them, then she ducked to the left and darted in front of it. Tires squealed. A horn honked, loud and long. She slammed both palms onto the hood and rolled over top, landing on her feet and taking off running. She heard the sound of cursing from behind her, feet slamming the pavement, heart pounding.

She remembered the direction Kai had told her Tesso's lay, so she ran the opposite way, her breath coming in harsh rasps, her pulse racing from the combined jolt of fear and exertion.

She was small and fast and though her pursuers could easily outpace her, she could duck around obstacles and vault railings with ease. She'd run drills like this all her life, planning for the moment they would come. So she zigged and zagged and ducked under low overhangs making it as tough for them to follow as possible.

The stretch of street was nearly deserted.

Safety in numbers. She needed to find more people, a crowd. They couldn't take her in a crowd.

No, not true. They *could*, but it was possible they wouldn't want witnesses.

But there were no people, only empty streets.

She could still hear them yelling at her, but their voices were farther away. She'd gained a tiny advantage.

She rounded a corner and ducked into an alley that

opened onto another street, but instead of running on, she darted behind a Dumpster. She looked around, feeling sick and afraid. The smell of garbage was heavy in her nostrils. The ground was littered with stained newspapers and paper cups. If her subterfuge was going to be successful, she needed to either tuck deeper into the space behind the Dumpster or climb all the way in.

Reaching up, she closed her hands on the rim and set her foot on the side.

And suddenly she stopped.

She was done with this.

Done with feeling sick and afraid.

Done with running. Done with hiding.

The men her mother called hunters had chased her from place to place, driven her from her home again and again. They'd cost her years with Kai.

They'd *killed* him, shot him on the beach that had been their place of love, their haven.

Kai was right. Running wasn't the answer anymore.

Dropping her hands to her sides, she tipped her head back and stared at the sky. The sounds of men running past the alley carried to her. They hadn't even stopped to look.

She took a deep breath. She'd let Kai talk her into coming to Toronto to find answers. She wanted them. Needed them. And she wouldn't find them hiding in an alley.

With a shake of her head, she walked out from behind the Dumpster, out the mouth of the alley, and paused, getting her bearings. Then she retraced her steps until she stood in front of the coffee shop. She could wait for Kai to return. Maybe she should. But she didn't know how long he would be and there was no guarantee that the hunters wouldn't return here as well. Besides, this was her life, her fight, and she was going to get her answers.

Kai would find her. There was only one place for her to go. Mentally, she mapped a route to Tesso's and started walking.

THERE WAS A BURLY GUARD AT THE DOOR, AND HE EYED Amber sullenly. "You a new recruit?" he asked.

"No."

The door behind him pushed open from the inside. A woman walked out, long brown-black ringlets tumbling over her shoulders. She was wearing faded jeans and a leather jacket with the sleeves pushed back to reveal a tattoo on her forearm. No, not a tattoo. It looked more like a scar, but one that had been put there on purpose. Amber couldn't see the whole image but she got a glimpse of wings extending on either side. The woman studied Amber, taking her measure, bronze-green eyes bright against dark lashes and dark skin. Then she glanced at the bouncer and said, "Enjoy the cigar."

He grunted as she walked away, her jacket swaying, offering Amber a glimpse of the knife sheathed at the small of her back.

The bouncer glared at Amber. "Go away."

"Tell Big Ralph that Amber Hale is here for a visit," she said.

If the guy's eyebrows rose any higher, they'd have been floating above his head. He pulled open the door and stepped to the side. "Back room," he said, his tone completely different, almost...deferential. Well, that was unexpected.

Heart pounding, Amber forced herself to stay calm, to scope the place as she walked through the main rooms toward the back. A guy behind the bar watched her with narrowed eyes as she passed but didn't stop her. The girl wiping down tables ignored her. On her left was a hallway that led to the bathrooms and, she was betting, a rear exit. She couldn't see any guards back there, but there was the bouncer up front and another by the door to what she guessed was the back room she'd been directed to.

His expression was blank as he opened the door to let her through, but he dipped his chin in a polite nod, which weirded her out. She noticed an ear piece, and she figured that the bouncer at the front had offered forewarning that she was coming. A ruckus behind her made her turn, and she saw two of the men who'd been sent to escort her getting a dressing down from the bouncer at the front.

Stepping into the room, she felt a drop in temperature and wrapped her arms around herself as the door swung shut behind her. There was a round table set to one side with an open bottle of scotch and three glasses. The lighting was dim. A single low-wattage bulb in a floor lamp cast a small circle of light around a man sitting crossed-legged on the floor in the center of the room. Around him were five flickering candles and a circle of what appeared to be salt. Before him was a stand-up mirror. He was lean and hard, and even though he was sitting down, she could see that he wasn't overly tall.

"Big Ralph?" she asked.

"My reputation precedes me." He turned his head toward her and his mouth shaped an ugly smile. Then he leaned forward and she saw him start in surprise as she stepped into the circle of light and he got a look at her face.

"You're…"

"Amber Hale. You've been hunting me for a long time."

"And you've been fucking hard to catch," he snarled. "From what I hear, you stayed ahead of three of my predecessors." He stared at her for a long moment, the seconds scratching by like nails on a chalkboard. "Funny, you don't look like you're a hundred years old."

So, he knew that about her. She wondered what other tidbits of information he held. She suspected he knew things about her that she didn't know about herself. A spark of fury pushed aside a bit of her fear.

She noticed then that his knuckles were split and scabbed like he'd recently been in a fight, and his face was weathered and lined, pouches beneath his eyes.

He was mortal. He could die.

And she couldn't.

This was what she'd been afraid of? This man who could bleed and hurt and die?

"What do you want with me?" she asked, taking a step forward.

"Don't break the circle," he muttered and gestured at the salt. Then he held up his hands, palms forward, and his expression shifted into a bizarre parody of sympathy. "Look," he said. "Parents and kids fight. I got a son, myself. Sometimes, I give him a shot to the head because it's the only way he'll learn. He gets pissed. He takes off. Then he gets over it and comes back. It's time you got over it."

An incredulous huff of laughter escaped her. "What are you talking about? You and your...predecessors have been hunting me for a century and you want to talk to me about your son?"

He blinked, looking nonplussed. Then he frowned. "You should just forgive him for whatever he did that pissed you off."

"Forgive who? Your son? I don't even know him." She felt like she was falling down the rabbit hole, head first. Or maybe she'd already landed on her head and this whole thing was a hallucination. Nothing he'd said so far made a lick of sense.

"Not his son." Kai's voice came from behind her. She spun, a convoluted mix of love and gratitude and relief buffeting her. He'd come for her just as he'd promised. And she hadn't doubted that he would.

"I told you to stay put," he said, his voice soft, his gaze intent as it slid over her features like a caress.

She was so glad to see him, it almost hurt.

"You're not the boss of me," she said and offered a small smile. He returned it, his dark eyes glittering in the dim light. "Did you collect what you were after?" she asked.

"I did. Safe and sound. Though there was some competition."

"Competition?"

"Might have been one of Xaphan's concubines. I'll look into it."

She didn't want to ask more questions, not in front of Big Ralph, so she kept quiet.

Big Ralph rose from the floor, his stance aggressive. But he stayed inside the circle. "You're in my place of business, soul reaper, sticking your nose into things that ain't your business," he said.

"Not your call to say if this is my business." Kai's gaze flicked to the mirror. "I have a feeling this is one time we can talk things out like gentlemen."

There was an undercurrent here Amber didn't understand, and it made her wary.

"What's going on?" she asked.

Big Ralph looked at the mirror, his hands lifting as he

shrugged. "Maybe you talk to her yourself? Maybe she listens to you?" he asked the mirror and then spun it to face her.

For a second, she thought she was looking at a reflection of herself. The eyes were hers. Hers but not hers.

Then she realized it was a young man in the mirror. And he looked like a tall, muscled version of...*her*. His chin was stronger, more masculine. His cheekbones more chiseled. He could be her brother. Or her—

"He's your father," Kai said softly. "The mirror's acting like Facetime with the Underworld. He's a demon. He can't come to Topworld unless he's summoned and slips temporarily into a human's skin." He glanced at Big Ralph. "But only the ignorant or fools would allow a demon access to their body."

For a long moment, there was only a roaring in her ears and a feeling of stunned disorientation. She didn't understand what he was saying. And then she did.

Her father. A demon. The demon of lust. Who ran prostitutes and drugs.

Palms slick, she spun to face Kai, then spun back to the mirror.

The image stared back at her, and he smiled.

She felt like her whole world was turning on its axis, while at the same time suddenly everything made sense.

How many times had her mother told her that her father had been evil to the core? How many times had she watched her mother burn herbs and incense, hang a horseshoe above the door, hang wind chimes, hang blue Nazar stones and even a mezuzah on the doorframe? Each time they fled and encountered new people, her mother came away with new superstitions that she added to the old. Or so Amber had thought. Her mother's machinations had always left her feeling faintly ill, especially when she added something new. With each chant and talisman, whatever home they inhabited had grown tight and small and Amber had felt like she needed to get out, leave, stand under the sun or stars. And now she knew why. They were designed to ward off dark spirits, negative energy, and demons. And Amber was half-demon.

"How long have you known?" she asked with a glance at Kai.

"With certainty? Only now, when I walked into this room. But I suspected when you held the darksoul on its tether. There are few beings that can hold spun energy like that. Soul reapers. Gods. And the highest ranking demons. Soul reapers are all male. Gods can't walk Topworld. Which left—"

"A demon's daughter," she whispered. Sin's daughter.

"My daughter," the image said, pride lacing the words.

Kai caught her hand and brought her fingers to his lips. "Amber," he said, waiting until she met his gaze before he continued. "It doesn't change who you are. It doesn't change anything at all."

But it did. It changed everything. She was a demon's daughter. She wasn't human. Not completely.

But then, hadn't she always known that?

She backed away from the mirror, from Big Ralph. From Kai.

Her mouth tasted like ash.

Her heart hung heavy in her chest.

Her lungs couldn't seem to draw enough air.

But Kai wasn't about to let her face this alone. He moved to her side and threaded his fingers with hers, warm and strong.

"My mother..." Amber wasn't even certain what she

meant to ask. Had her mother known? Of course, she had. That was why she performed her rituals, why they always ran. She hadn't wanted Amber's father to find them.

"Your mother was displeased when she learned my true nature," Asmodeus said, his voice soothing and rich, like warm cocoa. "She believed I would taint you, and she was determined to keep you from me. She was quite adept, it seems. I have been waiting a century to meet you, daughter mine."

"You sent people to kill me," Amber pointed out, her voice even, though she was shaken to her core. "And you wonder why my mother kept me from you?"

The demon's expression tightened. "I sent no one to kill you. They were to *retrieve* you. Bring you to me. Had you stayed in one place long enough to listen—"

"Stay in one place when they came for me with knives and guns? When not one of them stopped to explain or to say, 'Hey, your dad wants to meet you.'"

Asmodeus made a dismissive gesture. "They carried weapons only to subdue. They were human. You are not. What value were their weapons against you?"

"What value?" She stared at him, seeing the genuine perplexity in his expression. He was so far from human, he had no clue. "They terrorized my mother. Terrorized me. They kept me from putting down roots, building a life of safety and constancy."

"Such a life would have ultimately been detrimental to you," Asmodeus said. "Do you think your neighbors, your colleagues, your lovers would not have noticed your failure to age."

"It would have been my choice when to move on. Your thugs chased me from my home time and again."

"To no real adverse effect. You look well, daughter. You are intelligent, brave. You have not been harmed."

"Not been—" She pressed her lips together and got her temper under control. He was a demon. He didn't understand what she was saying. There was no doubt he truly believed his arguments. "Your men killed Kai," she said flatly.

"He is not dead now," Asmodeus said with a dismissive wave, clearly not seeing the problem.

Kai made a strangled sound that was suspiciously close to a laugh. She remembered using almost the exact same words to him.

"Why did they kill him? Why not just separate us and take me?"

"Convenience," Asmodeus said. "He was an impediment to your retrieval. And I happened to owe Sutekh a small debt. I paid that debt with Kai Warin's soul."

She stumbled back a step and her gaze shot to Kai's. He hadn't been wrong. All these years he'd blamed her for his death and he'd been right. It was her fault. Loving her had gotten him killed.

"Amber," he said.

She looked away, shaking her head side to side, sick, appalled.

"Amber," he said again and he cupped her cheeks and forced her to look at him. "Not your fault. Not any of it. And the outcome..." He grinned. "I like who I am, what I am. And we're the same now. Don't you see? If I hadn't died that night, how long would we have had? How long until you'd have been forced to leave me behind. You wouldn't have aged. At some point, you'd have run. Now, we have forev-"

"Don't," she said. "Don't say it."

"Not. Your. Fault," Kai said again.

On some level, Amber knew he was right. Not her fault. And given had things had turned out, maybe it wasn't so bad. That part she'd concede. But the rest of it...discovering Asmodeus was her father...that would take time to accept.

She stepped closer to the mirror. "You stole fifty years from us."

Asmodeus looked at her with eyes so similar to her own, and suddenly he looked ancient. His face was unchanged, but something in his expression reflected the knowledge of ages. "Your mother stole a century from me. I had no chance to know you. We will remedy that now."

"Will we? My mother had reasons she didn't want you in our lives. In *my* life."

"Reasons based on the superstitions of those around her and things she had been taught, false doctrines and such." He gave a negligent wave.

"How did she get pregnant with me? How did you even—"

Asmodeus lifted a brow. "One hundred human years and you do not understand procreation?"

She despised him. "I understand procreation just fine. What I don't understand is how you obtained a corporeal form, how you stepped through the mirror, how the genetics worked."

"Your mother was a supernatural. Not a full-blooded creature, but one with a supernatural heritage. Perhaps she was the offspring of one of Xaphan's concubines or a Daughter of Aset." He made a dismissive gesture. "I obtained corporeal form when a mortal summoned me and I inhabited his body. It was really quite simple."

"Why my mother?"

She was startled when his expression softened.

"She was beautiful," he said. "And she made me laugh."

Amber stared at him. Finally, she asked, "What if I don't want to know you?"

He gave a lazy, one-shouldered shrug. "I have eternity to change your mind."

A horrible thought. Eternity to avoid her father.

Asmodeus's gaze slid to Kai. "What payment do you wish, soul reaper? You have succeeded where all others failed. You have brought my daughter to me. You have delivered her. You deserve your bounty. State your demand, and then leave."

His words iced Amber's veins. She turned to Kai, feeling ill. What was this? Had it been his plan all along, to deliver her to Asmodeus for a reward, to—

She lifted her gaze to find him watching her, and his mouth curved in a wicked smile, white teeth flashing. In that second, her doubts evaporated. In that second she was ashamed of her mistrust. She knew what he was going to say before he said it, and despite the fact that her head was reeling from the revelations of the day, she was smiling back at him even before the words left him.

"There is no bounty that could match what I already have." His gaze held hers.

"If you have no wish for a bounty then why did you bring her?" Asmodeus asked.

"For her. To set her free." He leaned in and spoke only for her. "Do you see, my little love? There are no monsters under the bed."

"Oh, but there are," Amber said. "They're under the bed and staring at me through a mirror. There's a monster *in* my bed, one who rips out hearts. But they don't scare me. Not anymore. Turns out I'm half monster. And I'm done running."

Kai looped his arm around her shoulder and pressed a kiss to her temple. "You done here?" he asked.

"Yes," she turned away from the mirror and Asmodeus's voice rang out. "I did not give leave for you—"

"You going to stop her?" Kai cut Asmodeus off. "You going to force her to stay here and talk to you? You going to have your men confine her? That'd be an excellent way to create a relationship." He stepped closer to the mirror, as close as he could go without disrupting the circle, his voice low. "Give her time to process what she learned here today. Give her time to think. If you force her, you will lose her." He paused. "You spent a century looking for her. You found her. Do you want to lose her again?"

The silence stretched, and then Asmodeus said, "Amber." When she turned, he lifted an obsidian knife and slashed the tip of his index finger. Then he drew a heart on the glass in demon blood.

Kai made a choked sound.

Amber laughed. She couldn't help it. "Like father, like daughter," she muttered, then clapped her palm over her mouth, shocked that she'd said that aloud. Shocked that she'd even thought it.

Asmodeus smiled, not just with his lips but with his whole face, cheeks creasing, the corners of his eyes crinkling. "It pleases me to hear you laugh," he said. "Stay. Talk."

Amber shook her head. "No." Asmodeus's smile faded. "Not today," she added, and his smile returned, though not as bright as it had been before.

Holding Kai's hand, she walked from the room, through the club, out the front door. The sun was out, warm and bright, and she tipped her face to catch its rays as she and Kai walked hand-in-hand down the street.

EPILOGUE

"CLOSE YOUR EYES," KAI SAID. "I HAVE A SURPRISE."

Amber looked up from the canvas she was working on, her first canvas, her first permanent work, something that would last. "I hate surprises."

"Lie."

She laughed.

"You loved your surprise last night." He leaned in and nipped at the sensitive spot where her neck met her shoulder. Amber gave a yelp, and he smiled to himself as he pulled her to her feet and kissed her and she melted into his arms.

"Only because you were my surprise," she murmured. "I thought you couldn't come back until next week."

"Time off for good behavior." It was nothing less than the truth.

He hadn't known how Sutekh would react when he learned about Amber. But what could have been an utter disaster that led to Kai's destruction had, in fact, turned out to be a boon. Kai was mated to Asmodeus's daughter, and rather than see that as a bad thing, Sutekh had seen it as a political advantage. One of his soul reapers was linked to a demon, one that while not nearly as powerful as Sutekh, was a valuable ally.

That meant Kai moved up the soul reaper ladder, gaining a bit of security. Just like in a Topworld job. Next thing he knew, he'd be getting a picket fence and a dog.

Soul reapers were free to live in the Topworld and Kai was no exception, so being with Amber was easy. They hadn't yet asked Asmodeus if Amber was free to travel to the Underworld. Kai didn't think Amber was ready to know the answer.

But Amber had been thawing a bit toward her father's attempts to get to know her. Not much. But a little. She'd thawed enough that for their last visit she hadn't gone to Tesso's. Instead, she'd set up a mirror here at home and set her own candles and circle, summoning her father on her turf and her terms. Kai had left them to talk, and once or twice he'd heard her laughter through the closed door.

"Close your eyes," Kai said again, and Amber complied.

He led her outside, onto the street.

"Open." He couldn't keep the smile from his voice.

"That's your—"

"Mint-condition 1960 Corvette convertible," he finished for her. "Good as new, thanks to Nick at Custom Autobody." Then he pulled open the door.

Sitting on the seat was a massive bouquet of Gerbera daisies tied with a purple silk scarf.

"Happy first day of the rest of our lives, my little love," he murmured, and lowered his mouth to hers.

"Happy first day of forever," she whispered back.

He jangled the keys. "Want to go for a drive? Down the coast? Maybe Arizona? New York. Shanghai?"

Amber laughed. "How do we drive from here to Shanghai?"

Kai shrugged. "We'll figure it out."

"Absolutely. Anywhere." Amber hopped into the car and cast him a saucy look. "So long as we don't take the highway to hell."

End

Keep reading for a preview of Sins of the Soul!

Join Eve's Reader Group for the latest info about contests, new releases and more! www.EveSilver.net

Follow Eve on Bookbub!

If you enjoyed Kai and Amber's story,
please leave an online review of Sin's Daughter
to help other readers decide on the book.
Word of mouth is an author's best friend.

PREVIEW—SINS OF THE SOUL
PROLOGUE

HE KNEW ONLY DARKNESS AND PAIN.

Nothing else.

Not name or place. Not memories or dreams.

Rolling onto his side, he gritted his teeth against the agony that ground like glass shards into his muscles, his joints, even the marrow of his bones. Such pain was outside his experience. He felt as though he were starving, not just in his belly, but in the cells and tissues that formed him.

How long had he been like this?

Minutes. Centuries.

He had no way to know.

Lokan. A word without meaning sparked, then faded.

He reached inside himself, trying to form coherent thoughts. It was there. The wisp of awareness danced just beyond his reach. He tried to grasp it, to contain it.

Yes.

Lokan. The word *did* have meaning. His name. Lokan Krayl.

He had memories, a past that he felt he ought to know, if only he could scrape aside the layers of dust to find it.

He pushed up until he sat. At least, he thought he did. The place that held him had no such limitations as direction or space, and he was left disoriented, unable to differentiate up from down.

The place that held him.

Reaching out, he groped for the walls that were not walls, the bars that had no substance. Or perhaps he was the thing that had no substance.

He was a prisoner. He thought that he had tried to escape many times, and he had failed.

Panting, he fought against the crushing fog that obscured any spark of certainty. And then he saw it: a boat to cross the river Styx. A boat and a ferryman. There but not there.

So what *was* there?

He scrubbed the heels of his palms against his eyes. At least, he thought he did. He felt nothing save pain, endless pain.

"Push me, Daddy. Push me higher." The voice was sweet and high and happy. So happy. A little girl on a swing, squealing with joy as she flew higher and higher. His little girl. He missed her. His daughter.

But she was safe. Somehow, he knew she was safe. He'd done that one thing right. He had sent her to his enemies to keep her safe.

He frowned, certain that was wrong. But it wasn't. His enemies were the only ones who could keep his daughter safe. He'd sent his daughter to the Daughters of Aset.

Dana. Her name came to him with stunning clarity, so bright and wonderful it sliced through him, making him gasp. In his mind he saw every detail of her sweet face, denim-blue eyes wide and trusting and full of love.

They were together in the sunshine. They were laughing.

Then she was gone.

With a cry, he reached for her and found only darkness...and a spark in his core. A spark of memory.

There were others he cared about. Others he must warn. Dagan. Alastor. Malthus. His brothers. Cold dread unfurled in his belly as he thought of them. Dread *for* them, or *of* them?

Even in his confused state, he knew that made no sense.

He focused his thoughts on them, willing them to feel him through their fraternal bond. They had a connection, not a true ability to hear each other's thoughts, but an ability to sense when one was in pain or in danger or distress.

The knowledge made him cringe. They would have felt his death in vivid, brutal detail. Each slice of the knife. Each drop of blood.

Death.

Was he dead?

He thought he might be, thought he might have forgotten and just drifted here in the dark. How long? How long had he drifted?

Long enough that he'd forgotten his brothers, his father. His daughter's name. Until now. Now he remembered so many things.

He remembered that his daughter had been there the night they took him. That somehow he had saved her. He remembered that they'd taken him away, hooded, bound, his power held in check. By what? What would have made him, a soul reaper, son of Sutekh, the most powerful deity in the Underworld, so weak?

His own will.

He had chosen to give his life for hers. It had been the only way. He had saved his daughter. He had sacrificed himself to keep her safe. And he had spared her the horror of witnessing what they had done to him.

Faced with the same choices, he would do it again.

He remembered their hands. Gloved hands. Knives. Blood. The smell of it. The taste of it on his lips. His blood.

Now, he pressed the flat of his hand to his chest, certain of what he would find: a gaping wound, the skin stripped from the surface of his muscle.

But he felt nothing. Nothing at all.

Who had taken him? Who had marked him and cut him? He knew their faces, human and supernatural, alike.

Rage came at him, a bitter, burning tide. He had been betrayed by his own kind.

Gahiji.

The name echoed through his thoughts. And the face. He remembered him. Gahiji. His father's trusted minion. Such treachery. Sharp as any blade. Gahiji had been there the night he was tattooed and skinned.

He thought he could feel their hands on him still, their knives, cutting only deep enough to separate skin from fascia.

They'd caught his blood in an oblong bowl. The image was sharply inscribed, clean about the edges, far clearer than his other thoughts.

He could *see* that bowl, and the hands that held it.

A ring. A scarab beetle. He knew that sign...He reached for the knowledge, but it hovered just beyond his reach, curling away like smoke, replaced by the vivid image of knives. Two of them, the blades black, dripping blood. His blood. His pain. Dripping in fat, red drops.

Had his brothers felt his pain? Had they known?

He could not feel them. Not now. Not then.

There had been someone behind him. Someone watching. Who? He could not see, though he struggled and writhed. That voice. He knew that voice. Horror congealed in his gut.

Betrayed, yes. By Gahiji. But not only by him.

He thought of his brothers, and white hot panic flared.

Urgency made him move, made him cry out in frustration and—

The memories sputtered and died.

He no longer remembered names.

Not even his own.

Get *Sins of the Soul* now!

ALSO BY EVE SILVER

Dark Gothic Series

(Books in this series can be read in any order)

Dark Desires

His Dark Kiss

Dark Prince

His Wicked Sins

Seduced by a Stranger

Dark Embrace

The Sins Series

Sins of the Heart (Book 1)

Sins of the Soul (Book 2)

Sins of the Flesh (Book 3)

Body of Sin (Book 4)

Sin's Daughter (Novella, can be read at any point in the series)

Northern Waste Series

(Eve Silver writing as Eve Kenin)

Driven (Book 1)

Frozen (Book 1.5)

Hidden (Book 2)

Compact of Sorcerers Series

Demon's Kiss (Book 1)

Demon's Hunger (Book 2)

Trinity Blue (short story)

The Game Series (Young Adult)

Rush (Book 1)

Push (Book 2)

Crash (Book 3)

Join Eve's VIP Reader Group for the latest info about contests, new releases and more! www.EveSilver.net

Follow Eve on Bookbub!

ABOUT THE AUTHOR

(photo credit: Shanon Fujioka)

National bestselling author Eve Silver has been praised for her "edgy, steamy, action-packed" books, darkly sexy heroes and take-charge heroines. In 2015 she won the OLA Forest of Reading White Pine Award, her work was shortlisted for the Monica Hughes Award for Science Fiction and Fantasy (2014), and was both an American Bookseller's Association Best Book for Children and a Canadian Children's Book Centre Best Books for Kids and Teens (2013). She has garnered starred reviews from *Publishers Weekly*, *Library Journal*, and *Quill and Quire*, two *RT Book Reviews* Reviewers' Choice Awards, *Library Journal*'s Best Genre Fiction Award, and she was nominated for the Romance Writers of America® RITA® Award. Eve lives with her husband, two sons, two exuberant border collie/shepherds. And a snake called Ragnar.

Join Eve's Reader Group for the latest info about contests, new releases and more!

Follow Eve on Bookbub!

Find Eve online at
www.evesilver.net

9 781988 674254